WHERE THE DARKNESS HIDES

Duncan Thompson

First published 2017
by Rowanvale Books Ltd
The Gate
Keppoch Street
Roath
Cardiff
CF24 3JW
www.rowanvalebooks.com

A CIP catalogue record for this book is available from the British Library.
ISBN: 978-1-911240-64-8

AUTHOR'S NOTE

While the town of Raven's Peak is inspired by the surrounding areas of the Aire Valley, West Yorkshire, Raven's Peak police station and the characters within are works of fiction. Any resemblance to real life buildings and people is purely coincidental.

That said, as the majority of this story is set in a police station and many of the characters are officers of the law, I have researched police practice and procedure prior to publication. However, in the interest of the story I have bent many of these rules; some have even been broken. As such, this story should not be seen as an interpretation of the police force and the difficult job they face on a daily basis. In addition, Raven's Peak police station should not be seen as a reflection of the workings of a real-world police station.

Where the Darkness Hides is not a crime fiction novel; it is a supernatural thriller, a work of fantasy. Therefore, this should be kept in mind when reading.

Many thanks, and enjoy.

Duncan Thompson, April 2016

PROLOGUE

The moon, almost fat and full, sat suspended in the midnight sky. Although summer was making way for autumn, the air was still warm and humid. In the canopy of the forest below a male owl cried out for his mate, and his song was returned tenfold. Then his serenade was quashed by raucous laughter that rang through Druid Wood. The owl took flight from his perch and glided over an ancient monolith long forgotten by the descendants of its architects.

Into the clearing, where the stone altar had stood undisturbed for centuries, emerged a wiry, fair-skinned man whose hair matched his frame and complexion. He pushed his glasses back up the bridge of his beaked nose and smiled as he admired the tablets. In his hand he held a black plastic bag, which rippled against the man's body as something inside twisted and squirmed.

The man was not alone; from the trees behind him, four drunken young people — two men and two women — stumbled from the trees. The wiry man looked out of place with the others, who were well-groomed and sported the latest fashions and hair-styles.

The alpha male of the group gulped the last drops of his beer and threw the bottle into the trees. He then moved his arm from his girlfriend's shoulder and placed a heavy hand on the shoulder of his oddball companion. 'This had better work,' he grunted.

'Oh, it will work,' Oddball said, his voice brimming with confidence.

He approached the altar and slammed the bag down upon it. The contents of the bag let out a yelp.

He then opened the bag and pulled out a tabby cat. The feline hissed and spat as it was dragged from its plastic cell. Oddball pinned it down with one hand, but the creature still put up a fight, biting its captor's fingertips. From the inside of his tattered, three-quarter-length leather coat, Oddball pulled out a knife. It wasn't an ordinary kitchen knife; it was much heavier, made from iron.

'Where the hell did ya get that?' asked the other male, the beta.

Oddball smirked. 'Ebay.' He held up the knife and pointed the tip of the blade to the moon. He then began to chant rhythmically, speaking in an all-but-forgotten language.

The cat continued to scratch and bite, but the man was not fazed.

'What the hell language is that?' Beta asked.

Alpha slapped him round the back of the head. 'Quiet, you idiot! Let him do his thing.'

The girls remained quiet and held on tightly to their men.

Oddball, continuing with his incantation, now turned the knife towards the cat.

'He's not going to kill it, is he?' asked Alpha's girl. 'He wouldn't really need to kill a poor little animal?'

Alpha told her to be quiet, but then answered her question. 'He says we need to make a sacrifice, an exchange. You can't get something for nothing.'

The girl tightened her grip on her man in anticipation as to what might happen, her hand shaking against his chest. Surely, the guy wouldn't kill the cat. But then again, she thought he did look a bit unusual — like he could be a cat-killer.

Oddball now finished his incantation and lowered the knife. He held the blade under the cat's chin so that its edge was under the fur. He paused for a moment, took a breath and then slit the creature's throat.

The girls screamed and buried their heads into their boyfriends' chests.

'Sick!' Beta cried in delight.

Alpha told them all to be quiet.

The cat's blood poured from its lifeless body and flooded the altar, running over the edge and pooling in the grass below. And then there was silence.

The group stood there for a few minutes, bemused. It was Alpha who broke the silence.

'So, now what?'

Oddball pushed his glasses back up the bridge of his nose again. 'I don't know. I don't understand...'

'What do you mean you don't understand? I thought you had done this before?' Alpha stepped away from his girlfriend and gripped Oddball by the throat.

'I... I... Maybe I said the words wrong,' Oddball spluttered.

'Kick his arse, man!' Beta growled.

Beta's girlfriend began to shiver as the temperature dropped; she moved in closer to her boyfriend, and said, 'Can we just get out of here? I'm freezing.'

'Me too. Let's just go,' agreed Alpha's girlfriend.

The temperature continued to drop. The air was now almost freezing.

Alpha began to shiver too, loosening his grip on Oddball. Then he was hit by a smell of rotten eggs. He placed his free hand over his nose and mouth. 'Who guffed?'

A black hand emerged from the pool of cat's blood, followed by the rest of an arm, then a featureless head. The creature screamed like a new-born baby, birthed from the blood.

Alpha and Oddball took a startled step back towards the rest of the group. The creature had now fully emerged from the blood, its entire body smooth and ebony.

'What the hell is *that?!*' cried Beta, his lack of intellect struggling to find the words beyond something he had heard in horror movies.

The creature screamed and flew at Beta. It wrapped long, icy fingers round his throat and lifted him bodily off the ground. The girls screamed as they held each other, a quivering heap in a pile of leaves.

Alpha charged to his friend's rescue. He flung his fist at the creature, but his arm passed through it as if it were a veil of fog. He winced, an icy pain nipping his hand; his sleeve was covered in frozen crystals. He stared at his fist and saw that the skin was red and raw. From the corner of his eye he noticed Oddball drop the knife and turn to make his escape. 'Get back here, you freak!' Alpha cried.

But Oddball did not listen. He had the sense

to know there were suddenly worse things within the woods than the local jock and his punk friend.

Another creature crawled from the pool of blood and made its advance towards Alpha. Beta was still held suspended by the first creature. The more he struggled, the more it tightened its grip.

A third creature now materialised, followed by a fourth. The pair made their way over to the girls, who continued to scream.

When the sound of the screams stopped, Oddball stopped running and turned round to look back towards the ruins. The only thing he could now see was a black, swirling mass. Every other moment a cloud of black smoke would disengage from the mass and disappear into the shadows.

Oddball smiled as a sense of accomplishment washed over him. He placed his hands on his hips and chuckled. Then one of the smaller clouds swooped in his direction, so he shrieked and quickly fled the scene.

Sometime later that night, on the south-west side of Druid Wood, a young man was busy placing fireworks into the dirt as his girlfriend began to undress in the tent behind him.

1

Joe could no longer breathe as the Shadowman tightened its grip on his throat. The fingers of the creature's other hand now dug deep into his chest. He could feel its ice-cold claws scratching against his lungs.

He pushed a hand against the window of the car door, but he could feel his strength being drained from him; his hand slid down the length of the glass, which squeaked as his fingertips ran against the condensation. His vision began to fade and his head slumped forward until his chin rested on his chest.

There was a bright light, which Joe let wash over him, not afraid to die. He felt its warmth on his skin and he let his lips smile a little at the prospect that this nightmare would soon be over. And then he took a sharp sudden breath of air as the grip round his throat loosened. The intake of oxygen revitalised him. He clenched a fist and lashed out at the car door.

His vision returned in time to witness a cloud of ash erupt in front of him as the morning sunlight flooded the interior of the car.

Joe coughed and spluttered as the dust settled. Once he had caught his breath, he opened the car door and dropped out on to the ground. He lay on his back, his hand clutching at his cracked ribs, as he stared at the rising sun. When his eyes couldn't stand the brightness any longer, he closed them and drifted out of consciousness.

* * *

Joe didn't exactly dream — it was more like flashbacks were visiting him while he slept. At first he had images of being sat around a campfire drinking beer with his friends. Then the shadows of the woods seemed to take on a life of their own, clawing and screaming at him. And he was cold. The shadows had brought the cold with them. Finally, there were images of something pursuing him through the forest — something he couldn't quite see, something in the shadows…

Joe was woken by something prodding him in the ribs and the sound of sirens approaching. He squinted up at the hiker who stood over him, holding a walking stick.

'Are you okay?'

Joe raised a hand to shield his eyes from the sun, which had moved across the sky. Noon.

'Where's Tony?' was the most Joe could manage, before he passed out again.

* * *

Joe found himself standing in a cave shouting for his brother.

'I'm here,' Tony said from behind him.

Joe turned around to see his younger brother standing before him. 'Thank God! Are you okay?'

'I'm fine,' Tony replied, before bursting into flames.

Joe stumbled back a step as a shadowy creature lunged towards him from the fire.

2

Joe slowly awoke and an artificial source of light flooded his eyes. He squinted and placed a hand over his face while his eyes adjusted to the brightness.

Once fully conscious, Joe found himself lying in an unfamiliar bed. The sheets were white and rough to the touch. A needle, which was attached a fluid bag, protruded from the back of his hand. A series of monitors sat on a trolley next to the bed, emitting a gentle buzz.

Joe tried to sit up but a sharp pain radiated from his side, reminding him of the injury to his ribs. He reached for his side, and under his t-shirt he felt bandages tightly wrapped round his chest.

The door opened and Linda entered the room carrying a glass of water. When she saw her fiancé was conscious her eyes widened and she rushed over to the bed. 'At last, you're awake!' she shrieked, laying kisses all over his face.

'How long have I been here?' Joe asked. His voice was hoarse and his throat felt like sandpaper.

Linda simply brought the glass to his mouth and tilted it slightly, allowing him to take gentle sips.

The water was blissfully cool and soothed Joe's dry throat.

'I'll get the doctor,' she said.

Joe took hold of the glass and finished the rest of the water as Linda left the room. Within a few moments she returned with a middle-aged man who had greying curly hair and was dressed in a white lab coat.

'So, our boy is finally awake,' the doctor said. 'Joseph, I'm Doctor Callaghan. I will be your physician while you're here.'

'It's just Joe,' Joe muttered.

'Excuse me?' Dr Callaghan asked.

'Joe. I like to be called Joe.'

'Okay, Joe,' the doctor said as he reached over the bed. 'I'd need to do a few simple tests…'
He shone a torch in Joe's eyes and felt his pulse, muttering 'uh-huh' when he performed each action. He then picked up the clipboard that sat in a tray at the foot of the bed and scribbled some notes. 'Can you tell me your full name?' he asked, without looking up from the clipboard.

'Joe. Joseph Costello.'

'Good. And your date of birth?'

'The twenty-fifth of July.'

'Good, good. And who is this?' The doctor pointed to Linda.

'Linda Williams,' Joe replied, smiling at his fiancée.

The doctor made a few more notes and dropped the clipboard back in the tray. 'Okay,' he said, 'your vitals are good, and your memory seems to be in order. There are no signs of amnesia despite that nasty bump to the back of your head there.'

Joe reached the back of his head and felt the swelling underneath dried blood, stirring a memory of tumbling down a steep embankment.

The doctor continued. 'We've treated the

frostbite on your face, neck and shoulders — although I am at a loss as to how you acquired such wounds.'

Another flashback — icy black nails clawing at him.

'I've prescribed a course of antibiotics to fight off any infection that may be in the wounds,' the doctor went on. 'I have also prescribed you morphine and a mild sedative to help with pain. I still want to keep you overnight, just for observation, but I'm quite confident we can discharge you tomorrow.'

Joe reached for Linda's hand and smiled at the doctor, saying, 'Thank you.'

The doctor was about to walk out of the room, but then he turned back to Joe. 'Oh, I've just remembered… There is a gentleman outside who is very keen to see you. Now that I've given you the all-clear I'll send him in.'

Joe anxiously looked up at Linda. 'Tony?'

A tall, slender, sandy-haired man entered the room. He looked to be in his mid-thirties and was dressed in a navy-blue suit.

Disappointment washed over Joe when he saw the visitor wasn't Tony. However, he was not surprised to see the man who now stood before him.

3

'Francis!' Joe greeted the familiar face, but his voice was uneasy.

'It's DCI Wilson today, Joe. I'm afraid this isn't a social visit.' Wilson turned his head and coughed into his fist.

Joe could sense where the conversation was heading. 'Linda,' he said, his eyes still locked with the detective's, 'I can't remember the last time I had something to eat. Would you be able to go and get me something from the canteen?'

'Of course.' She knelt down and kissed Joe on the forehead and then slowly made her way across the room. Before she slipped out, she turned back and gave her fiancé a worried look.

Wilson pulled a chair up to the bed and sat down, his arms and legs crossed. His eyes scanned Joe, taking note of the wounds. He coughed again. 'So, where's Mikey?'

Joe shrugged. 'Honestly, I don't know.'

'Don't give me that crap, Costello.' He leant forward, his face only inches from Joe's. 'Listen up. We have had three reports of missing couples over the last two days. The last their families knew, they were heading to Druid Wood. We got the reports on the same day you, your brother, Mikey and that prick MacDonald went for your little retreat.'

'So, what exactly you are you implying?'

Wilson raised his hands, as if he were

surrendering. 'Hey, I'm not implying anything. All I'm saying is we've got reports of people missing in the woods. That's ten people to enter those woods in the last forty-eight hours, yet only one of them has come out. I've got my own mother beside herself, worrying about her youngest son. I've got MacDonald's parents asking questions I don't have answers to, as well as the parents of the missing couples.' Wilson crossed his arms again and leaned back in the chair. 'As you were the last person to see at least some of these people, I figured you might be able to answer some questions.' He grunted, trying to hold back another cough.

Joe sighed. 'Look, I'll tell you what I know. I want to help, I really do. My brother is also missing — remember?' He paused, reluctant to reveal the truth. 'Shadowmen,' he muttered.

'Come again?'

'We... we were attacked by...'

'By who? Who attacked you?'

Joe shook his head and frowned. 'It wasn't a person. At least... I don't think they were.'

Wilson's eyes widened. 'Are you saying some animal did this? Attacked my Mikey?'

Joe clenched his first, holding back his frustration. 'I don't know. Maybe. I have no idea what it was. But I know they weren't human — and they were dangerous.' He heard how ridiculous his words sounded as they left his mouth.

Wilson leaned forward again, and this time his nose pushed up against Joe's. He poked a bony index finger under Joe's chin. His breath smelt of stale cigarettes when he spoke. 'I never approved of Mikey hanging around with you and your wet lettuce of a brother. Your father was no good, and

I've always expected his lads to turn out much the same...'

Joe was a breath away from breaking the finger that poked into his chin when Linda returned.

Her interruption caused Wilson to draw back. He straightened his tie and cleared his throat. 'I've no further questions at this moment, Mr Costello. But if you can think of anything, please contact the station.' He turned to leave the room. 'Miss Williams...' He nodded as he passed her.

'What was that about?' Linda asked, once the detective had left the room; the sound of an uncontrollable cough echoed down the corridor.

'He's just worried about Mike. I am too — and the others.'

Linda placed a pre-packed sandwich on the bedside table. 'Joseph, baby, what happened out there?'

'I... I can't really remember. It's still a little fuzzy.' Joe was disappointed with himself for lying, but he couldn't face talking about the events in the woods. He rolled onto his good side and curled into a foetal position. 'I think I'm going to go to sleep now. I guess I'll see you in the morning?'

'What about your sandwich?'

'I've lost my appetite. I'm feeling a bit spaced out with all these painkillers they've pumped into me.' Another lie.

'Okay, baby.' Linda kissed his forehead again and began to leave. She lingered in the doorway for a moment, a finger poised over the light switch. 'I love you, baby.'

'Love you too. Oh, and babe?'

'Yes?'

'Can you leave the light on?'

4

By mid-afternoon the following day the Raven's Peak constabulary had sealed off the whole of Druid Wood, making the entire area a crime scene; blue and white tape was wrapped round the perimeter. To the south, on the dirt track where Joe had parked his car (which was now clamped in the police station car park awaiting forensic analysis) that fateful evening, Detective Wilson had set up a command post. Several police vans had arrived, as well as patrol cars, and a forensics tent had been pitched.

Wilson rolled out a map of the area on the bonnet of one of the patrol cars and marked out places of interest with a red felt-tip pen. Next to him stood a fledgling detective named Sarah Gladwin. She had only been with the police force for a few years but had risen to sergeant in no time and had been placed on a fast-track program to make her detective. She was a respected member of the force — and not just because her father, a retired chief inspector, was a legend among the officers.

Wilson nodded to Gladwin, signalling her to take the lead.

Gladwin called out to get everyone's attention. 'Okay,' she said, her voice unusually high, 'this is what we are going to do... I want you to split into three units. Each unit will search an area marked here.' She pointed and the officers peered at the map. 'We have four hours until the sun sets, which doesn't give us a lot of time to search the area. I want you to report in on the hour every hour regardless of whether or not there is anything of interest.'

This went without saying, but the officers were happy to oblige.

Wilson then took over. 'It is no secret that I have a personal interest in this case, gentlemen. I am confident you will give this task your utmost attention and perform to the best of your abilities. Needless to say, those who *do* perform as expected will receive a glowing commendation in my report and my eternal gratitude.' He covered his mouth and coughed into his hand, then wiped the mucus off on the back of his trousers.

A chorus of 'yes, sir!' and 'of course, guv!' erupted from the surrounding officers.

Wilson looked at Gladwin, his eyes naturally wandering to her ample chest. He quickly looked up again, hoping she hadn't noticed his glance. 'Back to you, Detective Gladwin.'

Gladwin ignored his gaze. 'Officers Campbell and Raimi...'

'Yes, ma'am?' they said, in unison.

'I want you to search section one marked on the map here.' Gladwin pointed to an area of Druid Wood which marked an old poachers' trail. 'Be careful, gentlemen. I am sure you are more than aware of the history of this area of the wood.'

The two officers nodded.

'Officers Craven and Englund, section two, please.' Gladwin pointed to the midsection of Druid Wood. 'Finally, Officers Carpenter and

Curtis...' She gave Curtis, the only other female member of the team, a smile of solidarity. 'You take —'

'Let me guess, section three?' Officer Carpenter interrupted.

Wilson glared at the rookie. 'Very astute of you, Carpenter,' he said, his voice dripping with sarcasm. 'You might make detective one of these days.'

Gladwin continued calmly, as if the interruption had never happened. 'Carpenter and Curtis, you take section three.' She pointed to the area of the map that gave the woods their name; an area where druids had once conducted their rituals in centuries gone by.

'Well?' cried Wilson, clapping his hands twice. 'What are you waiting for? Hop to it!' He coughed again.

As the other officers hurried across the meadow towards the woods, Detective Gladwin turned to her superior. 'When do you begin treatment?'

Wilson cleared his throat. 'My first session was supposed to be today, but I have postponed it until I find Mikey.'

A worried frown flitted across Gladwin's brow, but she quickly forced a smile. 'Don't worry, guv, we'll find him.'

Wilson stared across the valley towards the woods. 'I know someone who has a lot to answer for if we don't.'

5

Officer Campbell paused to catch his breath, removing his helmet and wiping his brow with the back of his hand. Although it was mid-October, the day was humid; the air was thick and heavy and hiking through the woods in the middle of the afternoon wasn't helping with the heat. 'Which way now?' he asked.

Officer Raimi, looking equally flushed, arched his back to be able to look his colleague in the eye. 'That way, I think.' He pointed to a trail that led in a north-easterly direction.

Campbell placed his helmet back on his head and gestured to Raimi to lead the way.

After several hundred yards they came to a wire fence, which ran as far as the eye could see in both directions of the valley.

'Well, how do we get round this?' Campbell asked.

Raimi scanned the fence and shrugged. 'Forget it — let's go back.'

'Wilson will go ape if we return empty-handed. You can wave goodbye to that sergeant's badge you've been chasing if you go back now.'

Raimi muttered to himself then spotted something hanging from the fence a few feet up the embankment. It was a tattered piece of denim. Raimi opened his toolkit and bagged it as evidence. He then noticed that the wires of the fence had been widened enough to allow someone to slip through.

Raimi tossed his kit over the fence and then clambered through the gap. Campbell followed, but his bulkier frame made it difficult to pass through as easily.

'Now where?' Campbell asked.

'I suppose we keep following this path,' Raimi said, and led on.

Farther ahead, just off the trail, lay a rustic shack. Upon closer inspection, Raimi saw that the surrounding undergrowth was broken and trampled. He pointed out the area to Campbell. 'Someone passed through here — look.'

'How do you know that?'

'Look at how the ground has been disturbed.'

Campbell sighed. 'It could have been an animal.'

Raimi raised his eyebrows. 'An animal? It would take a pretty big animal to make this much mess.' He jumped off the trail into the undergrowth. 'You coming?' he asked, looking back at Campbell.

A trail of dried blood led the officers to a metal object half-hidden amongst the foliage. They knelt down to find a closed bear trap. Clasped within its jaws, crawling with flies and other bugs, was a severed hand. Its skin was mottled and grey.

Raimi placed a hand over his mouth as he retched as the smell of decay hit him.

Campbell turned away in disgust. '*You* can bag that.'

'I don't even know how I'd get it out of the trap without losing my own hand,' Raimi said, reviewing the scene. 'We'll let forensics take care of it.' He reached in his kit bag and pulled out a plastic marker with the letter 'A' printed on it, which he placed next to the trap.

'Look,' he said, pointing, 'the blood is thicker here and leads away from the scene.'

'Yeah, and deeper into the woods.'

Beyond the blood trail the woods cleared slightly to reveal a man slumped against a tree with his back to the officers.

'Excuse me, sir!' Campbell called.

There was no response.

Campbell moved closer to see the man had been impaled by a wooden pike, which was suspended from the treetops. The deceased man's head bobbed lightly as the pike was gently rocked by the breeze.

Campbell turned to Raimi, his head spinning with dizziness and his stomach churning. 'Get on the radio. Get Wilson to get up here — now!'

And then he threw up.

* * *

'This is bull,' Officer Carpenter spat.

'Why?' Officer Curtis asked, stepping over a puddle.

'It's a waste of time. There's nothing here. Wilson is wasting resources to find his brother, who probably isn't even lost.'

Curtis slowed down as the ground dropped to her left. 'Careful as you come up here — there's a pretty steep drop. What makes you think that?'

Carpenter sidestepped to avoid falling down the crevice. 'He's been missing two days, that's all. He went on a stag do. The guy is probably sleeping off a hangover somewhere.'

'That may be, but Wilson calls the shots. Besides, what would you rather be doing? Rescuing a cat from a tree? This is about as interesting as this job gets around here.'

The officers entered the clearing where the stone tablets stood; the moss-covered granite towered overhead. Curtis walked over to the altar that lay at the centre of the stone circle and ran her hand over the cold rock, fascinated by the ancient architecture. 'Do you ever wonder how old this is?' she said more to herself, but within earshot of her partner.

'Who cares?' Carpenter replied, idly looking around for something that might pass as a clue. Something moved ahead, beyond the treeline. 'What was that?' he whispered.

Curtis spun round and spotted a shadow darting through the trees. 'Stop!' she shouted. 'Police!'

The shadow bolted deeper into the trees. Curtis gave chase.

After a few yards, Curtis found she was pursuing a man dressed in a tattered leather coat. Gaining on her quarry, she leaped forward and rugby-tackled the man onto a mound of fallen leaves. As he fell, he dropped a knife, which clattered against the stony ground.

Carpenter witnessed the knife fall as he stumbled into the scene. He kicked it out of reach and then helped Curtis pull the man to his feet.

'What are you doing here, sir?' the female officer asked.

The man pushed a pair of glasses up the bridge of his nose. 'Just out for a walk.'

Curtis tilted her head to one side. 'Do you know this whole area is restricted?'

The man shrugged.

Carpenter put on a pair of rubber gloves from his kit and picked up the knife. It was heavier than he had anticipated; its weight suggested the blade was made from iron. 'Can you explain what you are doing with this, sir?' Carpenter asked, not looking at the man. Instead he was drawn to the strange marking etched into the blade.

The man stared sullenly into space.

'What's your name?' Curtis demanded.

'No comment.'

'Well, Mr No Comment, I'm placing you under arrest.'

'For what?'

'Possession of an offensive weapon, for starters,' Carpenter snapped.

Curtis handcuffed the man, leading him to the outskirts of the woods and towards the makeshift base at the far end of the meadow.

* * *

Wilson and Gladwin stood over the body-bag that lay on the stretcher.

Wilson unzipped it and the lifeless face of a young man stared up at him from inside. 'Christ!' He grimaced and signalled to Officer Campbell to close the bag.

'You know him?' Gladwin asked.

Wilson puffed out his cheeks and spat out a mouthful of air. 'Afraid so,' he nodded. 'Charles MacDonald. He's one of Mikey's friends.' He took a packet of Nicorette gum from his pocket and placed one of the tablets in his mouth. After two chews, he threw in another.

Officers Carpenter and Curtis proceeded along the path with a solemn man in their custody.

'Who do we have here?' Wilson asked, still chewing the gum; a squelching sound emanated from his mouth as his jaw moved up and down.

'Don't know, guv,' Carpenter replied. 'We found him lurking near the old druid altar.'

'Well, did you check him for some form of identification, Carpenter?' The chewing grew louder.

'Yes, guv. But the only thing he had on him was this...' Carpenter held up the knife, which was now wrapped in a transparent evidence bag.

Wilson took a step back. 'Jesus Christ. Alright, take him back to the station and hand *that* in to the evidence tent.' He noticed the sun was beginning to set and then glanced at his watch. 'Gladwin?'

'Yes, guv?'

'You heard from Craven and Englund yet?'

Gladwin shook her head; a length of jet-black hair fell loosely over her face. 'No, not yet.'

'Call them back in.' Wilson sighed. 'We're going to wrap this up for today.' He spat the gum onto the dusty path and headed towards his car.

* * *

'Yes, ma'am. Understood.'

The radio hissed and crackled with static, but Officer Craven managed to receive the message. Officer Englund looked over to his partner, his eyes silently asking what their next move would be.

'Back to the station — they're calling it a day.'

Englund looked at the sky; the sun was deep orange and all but hidden under the horizon. 'Good thing, too. We won't be able to see shit in a few minutes.'

They made their way back to the base as darkness began to trespass through the trees, bringing an odd smell of sulphur along with it.

Englund put the back of his hand to his nose. 'What is that smell?' he said, gagging.

Craven screwed up his face. 'Dead animal, maybe?'

Englund shivered as the darkness set in. He thrust his hands in his pockets and jogged on the spot. 'Jesus, it was hot just a minute ago.'

Craven shuddered and gritted his teeth as a bitter wind nipped his cheeks. 'It's night-time now — bound to get cold.'

'Yeah, but not this quick, surely?'

'Getting close to winter now. Just keep moving, that'll keep you warm.'

The officers marched onwards but the air grew colder, slowing them down. Englund stopped walking, his whole body shuddering from the cold.

Craven turned to face him as the smell of sulphur grew stronger. 'C'mon. Keep mo —'

He abruptly stopped talking as he saw a shadow creep over Englund's upper legs and his torso. The shadow shimmered, then moved up over his neck, stretching out as Englund continued to shiver. Dark fingers sprawled out over his chin and lips and proceeded to seep into his mouth. The rest of the shadow followed and then it was gone, swallowed by Englund.

Craven then felt a tight, icy grip round the top

of his own legs. He looked down in horror to see a shadow cast across his own body. The shadow moved upwards, its form becoming hand-shaped as it did so. As with Englund, shadowy fingers stretched out over Craven's face and slithered into his mouth. He could feel something slide down his throat, freezing his insides as it made his way to his stomach. Craven felt dizzy and light-headed, and his vision grew dim.

And then there was only darkness.

6

Joe Costello ran through the woods, but his pace was somehow slow; his legs felt heavy, like he was wading through cold water. The harder his legs worked, the slower he seemed to move. Tony was only a few feet ahead — always a few feet ahead.

Tony stopped and turned to face his brother. Although he stood still, he continued to move further away the nearer Joe approached.

'We should have left when I said.' Tony's mouth did not move, but his voice echoed inside Joe's head. 'We'd still be brothers if you had only listened to me.'

'We will always be brothers,' Joe whimpered.

Smoke began to smoulder from Tony and then he burst into flames. From the inferno, a Shadowman lunged at Joe. Its icy hand gripped around his throat, the pressure growing tighter, as it hissed, 'I'm your brother now!'

* * *

Joe jolted upright, his eyes snapping open. It took him a moment to realise he had been dreaming and that he was at home in his own bed.

He exhaled and relaxed; beads of sweat rolled down his cheeks, dripping onto the bedsheets. His body flopped back onto the bed and he lay still for a moment, staring blankly at the ceiling. He then realised the room was pitch black. He panicked and fumbled under his pillow for the torch he had placed there. He pushed the button and a beam of light projected onto the ceiling.

All was still and calm.

He took a few deep breaths and held the torch between his knees. 'I gotta get a grip on myself,' he muttered, wiping the sweat from his brow and the back of his neck.

He turned his head to see Linda lying next to him. She stirred slightly but did not wake. She must have turned the light off when she came to bed. A feeling of annoyance came over Joe; he had told her not to turn the light off, but at the same time he hadn't told her why.

Joe got out of bed and headed down the hall to the bathroom, taking the torch with him. The energy-saving bulb flickered to life, illuminating the room. Only once it was at its brightest did Joe turn off the torch.

He washed his face with cold water and then cupped his hands, allowing it to pool in his palms so he could take a sip. Still shaken by the dream, he turned the tap off and gripped the sides of the sink, taking deep breaths to compose himself.

Joe turned to reach a towel and dried his face. He stared at his reflection for a moment in the oval mirror above the towel rack, and as he stared into his own eyes he could hear voices whispering in his head. He closed his eyes to focus on the words, but he could not make them out. Then a Shadowman leaped into his mind's eye.

Joe opened his eyes, catching the reflection of

his pupils contracting as he took a sharp, sudden intake of breath. He stood there while his heartrate and breathing settled and then grabbed the torch. As he reached for the light switch, he looked back at the mirror, in which his whole body was now reflected.

Something looked different.

He lifted his t-shirt and stared at the reflection of his bare stomach. 'Looking a little bloated there, pal,' he said to himself, running his free hand over the newly formed bulge in his belly. He shrugged and switched the bathroom light off. With the torch lit, he returned to the bedroom and climbed back into bed.

7

Joe was woken by a banging at the front door which echoed through the entire house. To say someone was knocking was an understatement; it was as though someone was trying to kick the door open.

'Linda?' he croaked, as he reached across the sheets.

Her side of the bed was empty.

Reacting to the cold space, Joe's eyes opened and then closed instantly upon seeing the sunlight flooding through a gap in the curtains. He rolled away from the light and opened his eyes again, focusing on the alarm clock which sat on the bedside table. It was 9.30am and the thumping at the door continued.

Panicked at not knowing where his fiancée was, Joe leaped out of bed, quickly threw on a pair of jeans and a t-shirt and ran down the stairs to the hall way. As he reached the foot of the stairs, Linda emerged from the kitchen.

'Who on earth is that?' she asked, jerking her head toward the door.

Joe grabbed his fiancée, gripping her arms above the shoulders. 'Where were you?'

The panic in his voice scared her a little.

'I… I was just out in the back garden.'

Joe hugged her tightly. 'I thought...'

The knocking at the door did not let up.

'Are you going to get that?' Linda asked, her voice muffled against his chest.

Joe released his hold on Linda and turned to the door. 'Okay, okay,' he said. He dropped the latch and opened the door a crack, peering out. When he saw who was standing there he swore under his breath then opened the door fully. 'What can I do for you, Francis?'

'DCI Wilson, if you don't mind.' Wilson pointed to the short, dark-haired woman standing next to him. 'This is my colleague DI Gladwin.'

Joe glanced at her then back at Wilson. 'Okay?'

Gladwin stepped forward. 'Mr Costello, please accompany us to the station —'

'Am I under arrest?' interrupted Joe.

'Not just yet,' spat Wilson.

Gladwin glared at her colleague and turned back to Joe. 'No, Mr Costello, you're not. We'd just like to ask you a few questions.'

'I've nothing to say — now please leave.'

Wilson pounded a fist on the doorframe. 'Listen, pal, we found your buddy MacDonald.'

Joe's mouth opened but no sound came out.

'Yeah,' Wilson continued, 'he's dead, and right now you're our only suspect.'

Linda stepped into the doorway and placed a hand on Joe's shoulder. Joe looked over to Gladwin, who once again glared at Wilson.

'I apologise for my colleague's tone,' she said, not taking her eyes from her partner. 'Yes, unfortunately we discovered Mr MacDonald's body yesterday afternoon. No, you're not a suspect, but we would like to ask you some questions and take a statement. It would really help with our investigation.'

Linda squeezed Joe's shoulder and then slipped her hand down to the small of his back, where she could feel a cold sweat seeping through his shirt. 'You should go... I'll come with you,' she whispered.

Joe coughed to clear the lump that was forming in his throat. 'Okay, just give me a minute to put some shoes on.'

'Of course,' Gladwin said.

Linda shut the door and turned to Joe. She wanted to say something, anything, but no words came to her. Joe clenched his fists and bit his lip until it began to bleed, trying to hold back the tsunami of emotions that threatened to overwhelm him. And then he could hold back no longer; he beat his fists against the wall over and over again, screaming as he did so.

8

Raven's Peak was only a small town — more like a large village really — with a population of around 15,000 people. The town itself was self-contained, surrounded by moorland with only one main road running straight through the centre. With a small town came an equally small police department. The building had once been a library, but was converted to the police station in the 1930s. It sat atop a hill overlooking the market, shops and bars that made up the town centre.

In the urine-soaked holding cell of the police station, Oddball paced up and down. He had been pacing up and down for the past fifteen plus hours and had yet to be processed. 'You can't keep me here! I know my rights!'

'Shurrup!' mumbled the town drunk, who lay on the bench at the rear of the cell with his arm slumped over his face.

Officer Campbell strode down the corridor whistling a tune he had had running through his head all morning (yet, annoyingly, he still couldn't quite place the name of the track or the artist). He stood in front of the holding cell. No longer whistling, he rocked back and forth on the balls of his feet. 'Alright, flower?' he said, looking at Oddball. 'You're up.'

The drunkard mumbled something as he struggled to pull himself up.

'Not you, Davey. Go back to sleep,' Campbell said.

Davey slumped back onto the bench and instantly began to snore.

Campbell instructed Oddball to turn round and place his hands behind his back.

'Well, it's about time,' Oddball said, doing as he was instructed.

Campbell unlocked the cell door and opened it; the sound of grinding metal hummed from the hinges under its weight. He then secured a pair of handcuffs around Oddball's wrists and pulled him out of the cell. He instructed the prisoner to stand against the wall as he locked the cell. He gripped him tightly by the arm, just above the elbow. 'C'mon, sunshine,' he said, leading Oddball up the stairs, out of the holding area and towards the interview rooms.

Coming along the corridor where the interview rooms were situated, in the opposite direction, were Wilson and Gladwin. They were accompanied by a tall, dark-haired man with an athletic build.

Wilson stopped and turned to Campbell. 'Put him in room three. And Gladwin...'

The female detective looked up at her partner, but she did not answer.

'Gladwin, you interview this long streak of piss,' he said, jabbing his finger towards Odd-ball. 'And get Carpenter in there with you. Campbell...'

'Yes, guv?' Campbell eagerly replied.

'Room one. I want you with me and Mr Costello here.'

'Yes, guv.'

As Joe and Oddball passed each other, their eyes locked and a short-lived staring contest took place, only broken by Oddball being pushed in to the interview room. Joe shivered inexplicably.

There was nothing obviously intimidating about the man, after all; he had a small, thin frame and a weak jawline. Add his long blond hair into the mix, and one could say he looked very feminine. If it weren't for the wisps of facial hair, Joe would have been convinced it was a woman being frogmarched down the corridor. No… it was the man's eyes that sent a shiver down Joe's spine. They were cold and menacing, and the blue irises were so dark they were almost black. And, as Joe had stared into these black pools, a sensation of being lost overcame him. In that one moment, Joe had briefly forgotten about his brother. It was that momentary lapse that scared Joe the most.

He shook his head and dismissed the sensation as he stepped into the other interview room.

9

Adam Barons, the young man always referred to as Oddball, sat with his head slumped and his chin resting on his chest; his hands, still cuffed, rested on the table before him, fingers interlinked.

'No comment,' he said, in response to the question Gladwin threw at him.

Detective Gladwin sighed and leaned back in her chair. 'So, you can't tell me why you trespassed while we were conducting an official police investigation?'

'No comment.'

Carpenter stood next to the door behind his superior, his arms folded. He glanced over the man he had arrested the evening before. Peering out from under Barons' left sleeve, an occult symbol was tattooed on his wrist. The officer could also see the same symbol on the blade wrapped in a transparent evidence bag — the same blade Barons had been arrested for possessing.

'What does all that mean? All those symbols?' asked Carpenter, pointing to the weapon.

For the first time since he had entered the interview room, Barons looked up. But he still did not answer.

'What? No comment?' Carpenter scoffed. 'I thought you would have known, see, as you've got it tattooed on your wrist.'

Barons withdrew his hands, but Gladwin

caught his wrist before he could hide it under the table. She pulled back Barons' sleeve; the tattoos went all the way down his forearm to his elbow. Gladwin pulled back the sleeve on his other arm and the tattooed pattern repeated. She glanced back and forth several times between the blade on the table and the prisoner's arms. There was no doubt that the markings on the blade and the tattoos were the same, even though she had no clue what they meant.

'So, I'll ask you again,' she said, as she thrust Barons' arms towards his chest. 'What were you doing in Druid Wood last night? And why were you carrying *that*?'

Barons removed his glasses, carefully polished the lenses on his shirt and then stared at Gladwin as he pushed them back onto his nose. He leaned back, his arms now folded across his stomach. 'And I'll tell you again,' he said slowly, 'no comment.'

* * *

Joe looked around the interview room. To his left was a two-way mirror that took up most of the length and height of the wall. He envisaged two sleep-deprived detectives sat on the other side, chain smoking and drinking strong black coffee while watching his every move — just like in a movie.

The remaining walls were blank with the exception of an ordinance map tacked to the plaster behind him. There were no windows in the room; the only sources of light were the florescent tube, which emitted a low hum overhead, and the glow of the exit sign that hung above the only door.

Joe had been told he was not under arrest, but the claustrophobic atmosphere of the room sure made him feel like he was.

Wilson sat across from him, coughed into a handkerchief, and then dropped two pieces of Nicorette gum into his mouth. He straightened his tie and switched on the tape recorder, which sat on the table. Campbell stood next to the door, his hands behind his back as he rocked on the balls of his feet.

The tape recorder clicked once and then whirred as the tape began to turn.

'Interview commences —' Wilson glanced at his watch '— 12.32pm. I, DCI Francis Wilson, am leading the interview. Present is Officer James Campbell. The suspect...' He paused for a moment to correct his words. 'The *witness* is Mr Joseph Costello.'

Joe flinched a little at being called Joseph.

'So, Mr Costello, let's start from the beginning...'

10

Sergeant Crompton sat behind the reception desk. He was six months away from retirement and this had been his post for the past five years. The underside of his jaw itched beneath his thick grey beard.

The young blonde lady still sat in the foyer by the public notices board. Her bony legs jiggled anxiously. She had come in shortly after Wilson and Gladwin had returned to the station with a person of interest, and she'd asked how long they would be with her fiancé.

The desk sergeant had answered bluntly by saying, 'How long's a piece of string, love?' He had then felt a pang of guilt from the glib remark and given her a warm smile. 'Honestly, I don't know. These things take time. I wouldn't like to guess, pet.'

The woman had insisted on staying and waiting for her fiancé, of course.

Suddenly, the door to the interview rooms opened and the blonde lady jumped up, only to sit back down, deflated, when a uniformed female police officer emerged with an elderly lady.

Officer Curtis escorted the pensioner through the automatic doors, which were the only way in and out of the station. 'We'll be in touch as soon as we hear anything, Mrs Smith.'

'Thank you, dear. Thank you.' Mrs Smith placed

her hand on Curtis' elbow and then doddered down the disability ramp, clutching onto the handrail.

Curtis sighed as she pinched the bridge of her nose; she could feel a migraine beginning to develop. She returned to the reception desk and slammed her head down on it — an act that only made her migraine worse.

Crompton chuckled. 'Let me guess, grand theft auto?'

Curtis groaned. 'A missing cat.' She massaged her left temple and sighed. 'I think Carpenter was right; this job is bull. At least in this town it is, anyway.' She looked up at Crompton. 'You know why I joined the service? To make a difference to people's lives — not to chase missing cats.'

'Well, speaking of your pal Carpenter, he is in interview room one with that feminine feller you arrested last night.'

'Goddamnit!' Curtis kicked the desk. 'That was *my* arrest.' She grunted, turned round to lean against the wood and then noticed the woman sat in the foyer. 'Who's blondie?'

He shrugged. 'Don't know, she came in shortly after Wilson and Gladwin returned. Think it's her feller Wilson is probably going to town on right about now.'

'How long has she been sat there?'

'Best part of an hour.'

* * *

Linda looked up to see a cup of vending-machine coffee in front of her face.

'I thought you could use this,' said the young female officer holding it.

Linda took the coffee and thanked the officer, who asked, 'Mind if I sit down?'

Linda silently shook her head and moved her handbag to make space.

Curtis sat down, extending her hand. 'I'm Officer Curtis — but call me Stacey.'

Linda shook Curtis' hand. 'Linda Williams…' She smiled and then took a sip of her weak coffee.

Curtis glanced over the reception. 'I hear you're waiting for your fiancé.'

Linda nodded. 'Yes — Joseph. He is giving a witness statement.'

'In connection with the recent disappearances?'

Linda nodded. 'Yes. I think so. His brother and friends disappeared in Druid Wood. Joe won't say what happened, but he hasn't been himself since they found him.' A tear began to trickle down her cheek. 'Apparently one of his friends is dead.' The tears finally won and Linda buried her head in her hands.

Curtis took a tissue from her pocket and handed it to the distraught woman.

Linda blew into it and wiped her eyes. 'Joseph didn't kill anyone. I know him — he is the kindest man I've ever known.'

Curtis nodded.

'Something happened to them in the woods. He won't tell me. Maybe he is ashamed or too scared to talk about it, but I know he didn't hurt anyone.'

The police officer placed her arm around the woman. 'Let me make some enquires. I'll try and see how long they expect to be.'

'Thank you.'

As Curtis stood up, the automatic doors slid

open and Officers Craven and Englund entered. The pair of them looked like they had had a heavy night of drinking; their skin was pale and their lower eyelids were black and swollen.

'Afternoon, gents,' Curtis said, accompanying them to reception.

They didn't respond. She then noticed that both their uniforms were filthy; mud was splattered up their trouser legs and dirt was streaked across their chest. But that had been known to happen, whether it was chasing a shoplifter through a muddy back alley or canvassing a boggy rural area.

The two officers walked behind the reception. Crompton glanced up at the clock on the wall. 'You're late for your shift, lads.'

They didn't respond; they simply pressed on though the double doors behind the reception desk and into the staff area.

The sunlight that shone through the windows of the foyer began to fade as storm clouds began to gather. Thunder rumbled in the distance.

11

Gladwin sighed and shook her head. 'Interview terminated at 2.47pm.' She switched off the tape recorder.

'Does this mean I can go home now?' Barons asked, rolling his eyes.

Gladwin's gaze didn't leave Barons' face as she said, 'Officer Carpenter?'

'Yes, Officer Gladwin?' Carpenter answered.

'Please take Mr Barons back to his cell.'

'With pleasure.'

Barons jumped up, tipping over his chair. 'You can't hold me here against my will, man!' He slammed his fist down on the table. 'I know my *rights*. You can't hold me any longer than twenty-four hours without charging me — and you've got squat on me.'

Gladwin nodded. 'You are correct. But by my reckoning we can hold you for another five hours at the least.'

'You bitch,' he spat.

Carpenter placed a heavy hand on Barons' shoulder and escorted him out of the interview room back towards the holding cells.

Gladwin puffed out her cheeks and made a popping sound with her lips. 'He's right,' she muttered to herself as she picked up the knife, examining it through the plastic evidence bag. 'We have absolutely nothing on this guy — nothing to connect him to any of this.'

Fair enough, the guy had been caught with an offensive, yet very unusual weapon in a police crime scene, but there was nothing to link him to the death of Charlie MacDonald, which, mulling over further, looked like nothing more than a tragic accident. The only person with any real connection to the whole mess was being interviewed across the hall.

* * *

'And you expect me to believe any of that?' scoffed Wilson.

Joe sat with his head in his hands. 'I know how it sounds, but it's what happened. I don't know what else to tell you.'

'Shadows coming to life and attacking people... You don't believe any of this, do you, Officer Campbell?'

Campbell shook his head. 'No, guv.'

'People don't spontaneously combust, do they?'

'Actually, guv...' Then the officer thought better than to draw his boss' attention to the phenomena of spontaneous human combustion. 'No, guv.'

Wilson rapped his knuckles on the table. 'And another thing, Costello, if your own brother is also missing, why aren't you looking for him? Or do you think *he* burst into flames and turned into one of the...' He glanced at his notes. 'The, err, *Shadowmen*?'

Joe clenched his fists and gritted his teeth, but he felt more than frustrated; his stomach was beginning to cramp. 'As soon as I was released from hospital I came here and filed a missing person's report.'

Wilson looked over his shoulder to Campbell. 'Can you verify that, Campbell?'

'I'll look straight into it, guv.'

12

Officers Craven and Englund marched through the male changing rooms. They passed Officer Raimi, who was changing out of his uniform and into a pair of jeans and a t-shirt, glad to be off duty. 'Alright, lads?' he said, raising a hand to his two colleagues.

There was no response; they continued to walk to the far end of the locker room and towards the stairwell that led to the basement.

Raimi shrugged. 'Suit yourselves.'

Once in the basement, Englund picked up a fire axe that was mounted to the wall. The pair headed to a utility room in which the fuse boxes for the station's entire electrical system were housed. Englund lifted the axe above his head and, without hesitation, brought it down upon the first of the fuse boxes. Sparks flew into the faces of the officers, burning their cheeks. Neither of them flinched.

* * *

Joe gritted his teeth as the cramps in his stomach worsened. He wrapped his arms around his belly; it felt even more bloated than last night and was now almost solid.

Wilson leaned back and tilted his head, as if backing away from a stick of dynamite, unsure if it was going to blow or not. 'You okay?' he asked, and for the first time there appeared to be genuine concern in his voice.

'Yeah...' Joe grimaced. 'They said I might get a stomach-ache as a side effect of the painkillers they put me on for my ribs.'

The pain, as sharp and intense as it was, quickly passed, but the bloated feeling remained. And then the light above them flickered.

All three men looked up as the fluorescent tube blinked and pinged. And then it went out. The room almost fell into pitch black darkness, except for the dull glow of the exit sign.

'Christ, now what?' Wilson cursed.

'Looks like the power's out, guv,' Campbell said.

'Yes, thank you, Officer Campbell, I can see that!'

Joe's heart raced and beads of cold sweat formed on his brow and under his arms as darkness engulfed the room. There was no torch in here to protect him. His breathing became heavy and erratic and his hands twitched nervously. Wilson stood; the high-pitched squeal of his chair scraping on the floor made Joe jump.

'Campbell, come with me,' Wilson ordered. 'Let's see what the bloody hell's going on.' He turned to where Joe was sat, his face only just visible, illuminated by the glow of the sign. 'You, stay here.' He left the room and Campbell followed.

The door closed and Joe heard the clunk of the ball bearings drop as the door was locked from the outside.

'Guv, are you sure he's our man?' Campbell asked reluctantly, as they headed through the dark corridors of the station towards the reception area. The only source of light was the dull glow from the exit signs above the doors.

'No. No I'm not, Campbell, but I got half a dozen parents out there wanting answers. The media is out for blood. We need to give them something.'

'But what happens if he is innocent?'

'Well, maybe he is... but the evidence doesn't look good, does it?' Wilson stopped and sighed. 'Look, if you want truth and justice, go join the Avengers. This is the police service; we need to be seen as *proactive*, we need to be *doing something*. You'll go far if you can learn the politics of it all.'

* * *

With all of the fuse boxes now destroyed, Englund dropped the axe. He and Craven stood still in the darkness for a moment and then they dropped to the floor. Their bodies convulsed and a black liquid was coughed up from their lungs. Then, simultaneously, they both burst into flames. The fire raged and then died down, leaving nothing left of the two policemen but scorch marks on the concrete floor.

Where the officers had stood two Shadowmen floated above the scorch marks, their faces featureless and their bodies smooth and black like obsidian. They turned to each other, screamed and then levitated into the air vents above, leaving behind them a smoggy vapour trail and icicles hanging from the shaft.

* * *

Gladwin was returning to the interview rooms after depositing the blade back into the evidence lock-up when she bumped into Wilson and Campbell as they stepped out into the corridor.

'Wilson, what's going on?' she said.

Wilson didn't reply; instead, Campbell spoke for his superior. 'Been a power cut.'

Gladwin frowned. 'I can see that.' She turned to Wilson. 'Guv, what's happening?'

'I don't know, but as it says on my badge that I'm a detective I thought I'd do some *detective* work and find out. Where is Carpenter? And that skinny feller he brought in?'

Gladwin was taken aback by his response and immediately felt kicked back into her place in the pecking order. 'Officer Carpenter escorted Mr Barons back to the holding cells.'

'Good,' said Wilson. 'Hopefully he locked Mr Barons back up before the power went. The last thing we want is a suspect running free around here. Not that I think that bloke can do much damage.' He paused. 'Campbell, head down to the cells and bring Carpenter back to the foyer. If the power's out it means the automatic doors are out too, so we're stuck in here. I want everyone to regroup in the foyer so we can do a head count. I need to know who is locked in and who is locked out. Gladwin, you're with me.'

Campbell raised his hand like a schoolboy requesting permission to leave class to go to the toilet.

'Yes?' Wilson said, with a sigh.

'What about that Costello feller?'

'He's locked in interview room three. He can stay there for the time being.'

Campbell nodded and headed down the corridor back in the direction he had come from. Wilson and Gladwin continued on towards reception.

* * *

Joe paced up and down the length of the interview room. The pain in his stomach had returned with a vengeance. He clutched at his belly; it felt round and bulbous, and even more solid than a few moments ago. Joe could no longer feel the contours of his abs. Then, underneath the skin, something moved.

13

Wilson burst into the foyer and marched over to the enquiry desk. Gladwin followed.

'Detectives,' Crompton said. 'A bit of a pickle we have here, isn't it?'

Wilson nodded. 'Indeed it is. Sergeant, can I have today's roster?'

Crompton shuffled through some papers that were pinned to a noticeboard behind the desk. He pulled down the rota and handed it to Wilson.

Wilson glanced over the sheet. 'We're a bit thin on the ground today, aren't we?'

'Cutbacks, sir,' Crompton said.

'Right. Where are Englund and Craven? According to this their shift started three hours ago, but I haven't seen either of them.'

'They turned up about twenty minutes ago,' the desk sergeant said. 'But I haven't seen them since.'

'Okay.' Wilson looked up from the rota, chewing his gum more vigorously now. 'And what about Raimi? His shift finished about half an hour ago. Did you see him leave?'

'Excuse me, Detective Wilson?' said a nervous voice from behind him.

Wilson ignored the voice and prompted Crompton to speak.

'No, I don't think so, sir. I think he —'

'Excuse me, Francis!' said the voice, now strong and confident.

Wilson turned. 'Oh, it's you, Mrs Costello.'

'I'm still Miss Williams, thank you very much.' Linda stood there angrily, her head slanted, her hands on her hips. 'But I would like to know how long you're going to keep my husband-to-be.'

'Look, Miss Williams, as you can probably tell we have a bit of a situation here. But if you must know I have a few more questions I'd like to ask your *husband-to-be,* and if we don't sort this mess out we are all going to be here a hell of a lot longer.'

* * *

Raimi fumbled through his bag for his mobile phone. The locker room had no external source of light and was now in complete darkness. His fingers touched the phone, which was resting at the bottom of the bag. He pulled it out and unlocked the screen, emitting a faint glow. It was by no means perfect, but it helped the young officer to see where he was going and prevented him from smashing his shins on the wooden benches that ran the length of the room.

He picked up his bag, shivering as he did so. An icy draught blew from the air vent behind him, causing the hairs on the back of his neck to stand on end and his skin to prickle. Then he lifted a hand to his nose as a rotten smell hit his nostrils. He lifted the same arm above his head and sniffed his armpit. No, the smell wasn't him.

'How many times do I have to tell people not to leave their lunch in their locker?!'

The temperature of the room dropped further.

Raimi put the bag back down and rummaged for his coat. 'Great, first the power went out and now the air-con is on the fritz. These budget cuts are going to be the death of me.' He was beginning to wish he hadn't nominated himself to be a union representative.

He dropped the phone on the bench in order to put on his coat. The phone lay idle and the screen automatically locked, killing the only light in the room.

Raimi reached for his phone and something sharp scratched the back of his hand; frost nipped at the wound. The officer flinched and let out a yelp as he brought his arm to his chest, cradling the wound with his other hand, 'Goddamn rats now, too!'

Stepping back, his feet slipped from under him; his head collided with the steel locker as he fell. Lying on his back, Raimi could feel that the floor underneath him had iced over. He tried to pick himself up but his feet kept slipping. And that smell — the stench of rotten eggs — was now even stronger.

Raimi reached up and pulled himself onto the nearest bench, his weight spreading over the wooden slats. Something cold suddenly pushed the back of his head into the beams, smashing his teeth. The force caused his skull to ricochet back, whiplashing his neck.

Raimi belly-flopped to the floor and rolled painfully onto his back as the taste of copper filled his mouth. He felt something cold slowly spread over him. His head spun and there was a ringing in his ears.

The moment before Officer Raimi lost consciousness, he could have sworn he saw a shadow standing over him.

14

Wilson ended the call and put his mobile phone back into his trouser pocket. He reached to the inside pocket of his jacket for a packet of cigarettes. The pocket was empty except for half a packet of Nicorette. The gum had held his cravings at bay for the best part of a month — well, either that or it was down to the shock of his diagnosis. But now he badly needed a cigarette.

What little remained of the Raven's Peak constabulary now stood around their commanding officer. Campbell and Carpenter had returned to the foyer just as Wilson had dialled the commissioner's office and now they eagerly waited to hear what their next move was.

'Listen up,' Wilson began, pulling himself up to sit on the reception desk. 'I have spoken to the commissioner. Because no one is hurt, there is no real risk of danger and we have only two prisoners, who aren't exactly on the most wanted list, our situation is not being treated as high priority. She said it could take up to twelve hours to send an engineer over here to get these doors open from the outside. Any emergency calls for our jurisdiction will be dealt with by the neighbouring constabularies. Saying this, personally, I'm in no mood to sit here and wait.'

'What are you proposing, guv?' said Campbell, raising his hand.

'Glad you asked. I want you and Carpenter to look for Raimi, Englund and Craven. In theory, they're all still here somewhere. Go find them and bring them back here. Sergeant Crompton?'

Crompton, who was slumped in his chair, straightened up. 'Yes, sir?'

'I want you to head with me down to the basement and see if we can get the power back on ourselves. If this is just a blown fuse, heads are going to roll.' Crompton nodded to signal he understood and got up from his chair.

'Ladies — and that includes the soon-to-be Mrs Costello — I want you to wait here. Set up an HQ within HQ, so to speak.'

Officer Curtis stepped forward to protest the idea of her doing nothing. The police force was supposed to be an equal opportunities employer, but she often felt that her sex and her race meant she was overlooked for said opportunities. And now was no exception.

'Yes, Curtis?'

In the corner of her eye, Curtis caught Gladwin pass her a stern look that suggested now wasn't really the time. 'Nothing, guv,' she said, stepping back in line.

'In that case,' said Wilson, 'let's move.'

Linda had said nothing throughout the whole meeting; she simply sat leaning against the ledge of one of the windows, watching the storm clouds roll in and the daylight fade.

15

Joe's stomach had swollen further still. Even in the dim light from the exit sign he was able to catch his reflection in the two-way mirror. He looked like he was at least six months pregnant.

The cramps worsened; a white-hot stabbing pain surged through his abdomen, as if the muscles were tearing.

Hands shaking, Joe lifted his shirt and looked down to see his skin ripple. Then something from inside him pushed outwards. The shape of a small foot pressed against his skin and then snapped back like an elastic band. Next, the outline of a hand reached up from within his flesh. Joe watched in terror as it drew back as quickly as the foot had done. There was another shift inside his gut and the shape of an infant's face appeared.

Joe screamed. The colour ran from his face. He was drenched in a cold sweat and began to shiver with fear. 'Help me!' His cry echoed around the room. 'Somebody help me!'

There was no reply. The pain intensified and Joe's belly continued to grow. Stretchmarks and scars erupted on his skin.

Clutching at his stomach, Joe staggered over to the door, barging his shoulder into it. The dull thud echoed. He tried to force the door open again but the pain was now crippling, bringing him to his knees. The skin of his belly began to bruise. One way or another, whatever it was festering inside him was going to come out.

Joe crawled on his knees to the table and pulled himself up; his sweaty palms made it difficult to grip, but he persevered. His entire body shook with a rush of adrenaline. He looked at his reflection in the mirror and stared at the unrecognisable, gaunt face he saw before him.

He scowled. He instinctively knew that, even though he had escaped the woods, he had not escaped the Shadowmen's torment.

'You bastards. You dirty bastards,' he whispered.

With his remaining strength, Joe picked up one of the chairs and launched it at the mirror, which shuddered but did not break. Joe grabbed the chair again and struck the mirror once more. The glass shuddered again, but this time there was a rattle around the frame. On his third attempt, the chair finally broke through the mirror and flew into the room next door.

Joe picked up a shard of glass and gripped it so tightly that its edges sank into his palm, lacerating the inside of his fingers. He raised the fragment high above his head, his hand trembling. He stomach churned at the thought of what he was about to do.

He hesitated.

Then, releasing a primeval scream, he brought the shard down, imbedding it into his left side. With the glass buried at least half an inch deep in his body, he began to drag it over to his right side, cutting across his belly. His entire being felt like it was on fire and his head spun with dizziness. He could feel himself begin to pass out, but he couldn't stop the self-inflicted C-section until he knew whatever was growing inside of him was out.

As the glass shard cut through his belly, Joe dimly noticed there was no blood. Instead, thick black oil seeped from the wound and pooled on the floor by his feet. As the oil escaped, the swelling began to go down until Joe's stomach closely resembled its usual shape. The last of the oily substance slopped to the floor and only then did blood — red, human blood — begin to pour.

Joe dropped the glass and collapsed to the floor, landing on his coccyx. He sat there trying to hold the tear in his belly together, the warm, sticky blood oozing through his fingers. Before him, the dark, oily substance that had bled from him moved and took on a solid form. It was the shape of a small child. It was black and featureless, reminding Joe of the Tar Baby from the Brer Rabbit tale. But it wasn't the Tar Baby. It was undoubtedly a Shadowman — only this one had depth and dimension to it, rather than the two-dimensional paper doll appearance of the ones he had encountered in the Druid Wood.

The Shadowman screamed. Unlike the others, when it screamed an opening that resembled a mouth appeared in its head. When the screaming stopped, the creature imploded and a black puddle pooled on the floor once more. The pool slithered across the room and squeezed underneath the door, escaping the room.

16

'I should put a complaint in with the union. It's discrimination!' Curtis growled, sitting on the bench in the foyer. 'I've applied for my sergeant's exam twice now and my application has been turned down both times.'

'Did you get feedback on why it was rejected?' Gladwin always tried to be sympathetic towards Curtis, but she had her own career to concentrate on.

'I'm still waiting for the feedback from the first time. It's because I'm a woman.'

'*I'm* a woman.'

'Yes, but you're not a *black* woman.'

Gladwin cast the rookie a stern look — a look she had perfected at the age of twelve. 'That's shit, and you know it. Look, Curtis...' she began, but then her expression softened and she smiled. 'Stacey... you've got to learn to play the game. It's all about politics.'

'She's right,' Linda added. 'It's office politics. It's the same where I work, and that's just a call centre. I can't imagine how hard it is here to get noticed.'

* * *

Davy continued to snore; the dull rumbling sound filled the confines of the holding cell. Given the choice, Barons would have asked to be moved to another 'room'. But this was the only holding cell the small-town constabulary had to offer.

The snoring continued until Barons could stand it no longer. 'Oh, do shut up!' he snapped. He was seriously contemplating smothering the old guy in his sleep. He had even removed his jacket to when something darted past the outside of the cell, breaking his concentration. Whatever it was had brought an arctic wind with it. Then something moved about in the darkness again, and this time the smell of sulphur hung in the air as the ebony shadow hovered in front of the cell door. Davy snorted and choked a little as the smell hit his lungs, but he did not wake.

The dim glow from the exit sign above the far door emitted just enough light for Barons to make out the featureless face staring right at him. 'You're here,' he breathed, a wide smile spreading across his face.

His expression quickly turned sour when the Shadowman's hand passed through the bars of the cell and grasped his throat. It lifted him off the ground, its black claws breaking the skin.

'B-but I freed you,' Barons spluttered. He lifted his arms to shield his eyes from whatever horror he might witness.

The creature paused, taking interest in the black tattoos that stood out starkly against Barons' milky skin. Dropping the feeble man to the floor, the Shadowman spoke, its voice echoing inside Barons' mind.

'Yes, my lord,' Baron replied, gasping as he scrambled to his feet. 'Yes, it was me.'

The creature's voice continued to echo inside his head.

'But, I don't know how to... Not on such a large scale, anyway.'

The Shadowman screamed, and the resulting shockwave caused the prison bars to rattle. Davy snorted and rolled onto his side.

'B-b-but... Yes, my lord... I understand.'

Barons closed his eyes and held his arms out wide. 'I am your servant.'

The Shadowman passed through the bars and crept over Barons' body, slipping up his neck and entering his mouth and nasal cavity. Barons shuddered, his lips and fingertips turning blue.

Once the shadow was fully consumed, a dark cloud spread across his eyes then dispersed to reveal their normal colour.

Barons smiled once more. He picked up his jacket, rolled it into a ball and made his way across the cell to where the town drunk slept.

* * *

Wilson and Crompton stood, each shining a torch on the destroyed fuse box. Crompton laughed. 'Your daddy never show you how to change a fuse, detective?'

Wilson rubbed the back of his neck and the torch light caught a glimpse of the fire-axe which lay on the concrete floor. He then glanced back at the damaged fuse boxes. 'Well, we've got the room and the murder weapon. Care to take a stab at who killed Mr Power, Sergeant?'

'I always preferred Monopoly myself, sir.'

'I bet.'

A drop of icy cold water fell onto Wilson's balding head. He shivered and shone the torch upward. Icicles hanging from the ventilation shaft were beginning to thaw. Another droplet fell and landed on the torch.

'I suppose it gets fairly cold down here — especially now we're getting closer to winter, sir,' said Crompton.

Wilson wasn't convinced. 'What the hell is going on?' he muttered under his breath.
He turned back to the damaged fuse box and rubbed the back of his neck again, sighing. He had no clue what to do next, but he didn't want to leave the scene until a solution came to him.

Crompton shrugged. 'Looks like you need a good electrician, guv.'

This gave Wilson an idea.

17

After climbing through the rectangular hole in the wall of interview room three, where a two-way mirror had once been, Joe found himself in an observation room. His arms were wrapped tightly round his stomach in a futile attempt to stem the blood that was flowing fast. Splinters of glass nipped at the edges of the wound.

Joe slithered across to the door like a dying snake, staining the tiles with streaks of blood. He raised a shaky hand and pulled himself up, using the door handle for support. The handle turned and the door swung open under Joe's weight, causing him to fall face-first into the corridor.

He crawled along slowly until he found an unlocked door and then sat in the stationery cupboard, leaning against a filing cabinet. A small window allowed very little light to enter the room, but it was still enough to see by.

Joe pulled himself up and rested his shoulder against the cabinet to support his legs. On the chrome shelf next to him were boxes of pens, boxes of pencils, packets of paper, ink cartridges, plastic tubs of papers clips, rolls of sellotape and duct-tape, envelopes (in varying sizes), document wallets, rubber stamps, postage stamps, boxes of staples, several staplers and one industrial sized wall-stapler.

Joe picked up the wall-stapler and opened it. It

was fully loaded. He closed the top, and then lifted his shirt, holding it up with his teeth. He held the stapler against the tear in his stomach, screwed his eyes shut and squeezed the trigger.

Click-crunch.

He whimpered and stamped his feet from the unbearable sting of the first staple.

He was going to need at least nine more.

Click-crunch, click-crunch.

* * *

Campbell and Carpenter entered the men's locker room, standard-issue torches in hand. The beams dashed left to right, illuminating lockers, coat hooks, a drinking fountain and wooden benches. The heels of their boots tapped against the floor tiles, the sound echoing around the room.

'You know, I've applied for a transfer to Bradford South,' said Carpenter, breaking the silence.

Campbell looked at him. 'You got a death wish?!' He laughed. 'Why would you want to work a city centre beat when it's easy work here?'

'Easy work? *Boring* work, more like. Besides, your career is not going to progress on a rural beat,' Carpenter replied, lowering his torch to the floor. 'Maybe it *is* easy here, but it's a dead end; the crime rate is too low.'

'You make a low crime rate sound like a bad thing,'

'It is,' Carpenter replied. 'If there is no crime, there's no need for the police. Sooner or later they're going to shut these rural constabularies down and have the districts overseen by the wider police force. So, by applying for Bradford South,

I'm just delaying the inevitable. Besides, Raven's Peak is going to be the first to go. For starters, the building needs condemning. We don't even have any power. Not to mention our most experienced member of staff spends all day behind a desk creating rotas.'

Campbell chuckled. 'Have you ever tried to make a rota? It's no easy task!'

'And Wilson has no clue of how to manage a force,' continued Carpenter. 'We've spent a whole day on his personal vendetta. I'd hate to be in his shoes when the commissioner questions the expenses bill.'

The light from Campbell's torch fell upon a sports bag, which lay on one of the benches with its zip half open.

'Raimi's?' Carpenter said.

'Let's take a butcher's...' Campbell stepped forward and his foot slipped out from under him. All 250 pounds of him crashed down on the tiles.

The fallen officer groaned, clutching at his left elbow. Carpenter tried to contain his laughter as he strolled over to help his colleague up. His feet also began to slip and slide, but he held his balance and managed to steady himself. He shone the torch to the floor, which was covered in a thick patch of ice.

'What the hell?' Carpenter muttered.

Campbell pulled himself up, using the lockers for support. A dull ache radiated from his elbow and travelled up and down the length of his arm. He could barely move the joint.

Carpenter swept the floor with the torch light; ice circled the bench, creeping up its legs. 'Just what is going on?'

'Not too boring for you now, huh?' Campbell tried to smile but the pain in his arm turned it into a grimace.

A groan came from the steam-room. Hearts racing at the sudden surprise of the sound, the officers spun round, the light from their torches hitting the door of the room. It was hard to tell, especially in the limited light, but there appeared to be someone behind the frosted glass of the steam-room door.

'Raimi, are you in there?' said Campbell.

The only reply was the echo of his voice. They approached cautiously, careful not to slip on any more icy patches. Campbell's elbow throbbed, making it difficult for him to keep the beam from his torch steady. He switched hands and light darted from one side of the steam-room door to the other.

Silently counting to three, Carpenter pulled open the steam-room door. An overpowering smell of sulphur escaped the cubicle. He covered his mouth with the back of his forearm in an attempt to stop himself from gagging. Campbell, unable to lift his injured free arm, turned his head away while holding his breath. When he saw Officer Raimi slumped in the corner of the steam room he exhaled with exaggeration.

With the steam-room door open the smell quickly dispersed, but the temperature in there was certainly a lot colder than the outer locker area. They hurried to Raimi and crouched next to him. His lips and fingers were blue, there were deep scratches on his face and neck and his shirt was torn across the chest. Blood was soaked into the fabric, but the wounds appeared to have scabbed over.

'Ben? Ben, can you hear me?' Campbell asked, gently slapping Raimi's face. Despite the temperature in the room, his cheeks were red hot.

Raimi grunted.

Campbell felt the injured officer's forehead. 'Jesus,' he said to Carpenter, 'he's burning up.'

They brought Raimi to his feet, and, despite his semi-conscious state, he was able to steady himself. Aided by his two colleagues, he slowly hobbled out of the steam-room.

18

The last of the duct tape tore away from the cardboard roll as Joe wrapped it around his waist, ensuring the staples were held in place. The sting across his middle eased off, replaced by the return of the dull ache in his ribs; he couldn't remember how long it had been since he last took his painkillers.

Linda! Joe suddenly remembered his fiancée had followed the patrol car to the station and was here, somewhere, waiting for him. He limped slowly out of the storeroom, the skin of his belly tightening and pulling around the staples. He made his way back down the corridor, following the trail of his own blood. He was about to enter the reception area when whispering began in his head. He paused, trying to make sense of the voice. It somehow sounded familiar but he couldn't make out the words. He reached for the door handle but was instead overcome with an urge to turn around. He did and took several steps back towards the storeroom. The volume of the voice increased and became clearer; someone was calling his name.

He stepped through the fire exit at the opposite end of the corridor and began to climb the stairwell that was on the other side of the door. He paused again, remembering how that night in the woods the Shadowmen had known your name and would call you trying to lure you in; but their voice had been unfamiliar and strange. The voice he was now hearing, that rang through his head, was known to him. It was a voice he had heard countless times, a voice he heard every day, but he still could not place it. Joe continued to follow.

At the top of the stairs, Joe caught sight of a tall figure stepping into one of the offices that occupied this floor of the police station. 'Hey!' Joe called, running to catch up. He barged through the office door, ignoring the pain in his ribs and stomach. Stood in the centre of the room was a shining black figure. It was the tar-person that had crawled out of him! Not even an hour ago it had been the size of a small child, but now it was an adult the same size and build as Joe.

It turned round and a slit resembling a smile opened up on its featureless head. From where the smile had appeared, the tar-like substance of the creature began to retreat to reveal a human face — a face that, like the voice, Joe knew all too well. He was looking at his own reflection. The tar-like substance rolled back further, exposing a human body — Joe's body.

Joe stared at the doppelganger; its skin was paler than his, almost white, and the eyes were black, but apart from that it was a perfect clone. Joe opened his mouth to speak, but he was lost for words. He closed his mouth and then opened it again, but still nothing.

The doppelganger smirked. 'What's the matter? Aren't you pleased to see me?' Its voice was the same as the one in Joe's head.

Joe looked his double up and down; even in the failing light from the office window the likeness was clear. 'What *are* you?' Joe couldn't believe how stupid he was sounding but he pressed on with the question. 'Me?'

The doppelganger smiled a smile Joe had seen in dozens of photographs. 'Yeah, something like that — just a tad shadier,' it said as it began to walk circles around Joe. 'I'm the darker part of you, the part that doesn't know when to quit. I'm the competitiveness you have that clouds your better judgement, that doesn't listen to anyone else. And then there is all that anger and aggression, built up inside. Anger you have been hiding for years. Who are you angry at? Tony? No, not quite. Possibly your mum, for making you babysit him. But no, that's not quite it either. Your dad… it's cliché, but yes. However, it's not quite the fact that he left you. No, the darkest part that hides within you is not anger or poor judgment, it's fear — fear you will turn out just like him. That's the root of your evil, Joseph: fear.'

'You're not me! You know nothing about me. You're one of them! A *Shadowman*. This is just one of the mind games you pull. It's all lies!'

'Why would I lie? Would I lie to *myself*? You know exactly what I'm talking about. The part of you that wouldn't listen to your brother, the part that caused him and your friends not only to lose their lives but also their souls — that was all because you're afraid to admit who you really are.'

Joe staggered back, his stomach churning. He placed his hand over his face and screwed up his eyes, moaning, 'Tony and Mike are dead, too?' He desperately wanted this news to be a lie, but deep down a part of him knew it to be true.

'Oh, believe me,' his doppelganger said,

'they're dead. More than dead, as a matter of fact. The so-called "Shadowmen" fed on their souls like parasites until there was nothing left but a dark, empty husk. That's what the Shadowmen are; they're the broken, tortured souls of men. I suppose your friend Charlie had a lucky escape, dying before they could get to him.'

'And you're not one of them?' Joe was trembling and a cold sweat had broken out on his brow.

'Let's just say I'm a distant cousin of the Shadowmen. But, like them, I'm partially made from your soul. I'm the part of your soul that broke first. Remember being in the cave? A Shadowman began to feed on your soul, but you woke up. I suppose the pain in your ribs reminded you that you were still alive, still human. I wasn't strong enough to consume the rest of your soul — not once you were awake again — but inside you I found something better. I found blood.'

'Blood?'

The doppelganger grinned. 'Blood is life. And yours is very nourishing.' It continued pacing around Joe. 'The "Shadowmen", as you call them, are ancient — as old as mankind, in fact. Like all old people, they are stuck in their ways. Ages ago, souls were pure and provided plenty of nourishment. And the Shadowmen craved what they once were. But these days souls are weak and corrupt; they burn out too easily. Blood, on the other hand... I could have stayed inside you for a very long time, feeding from your blood. It would have sustained me a lot longer than your soul. But, your subconscious put up a fight and started kicking me out.'

'And now what?'

'Now, I need to find a new host. I might start with that slim blonde you love...'

Joe lunged forwards, fists flying. As his knuckles connected, the doppelganger imploded. The resulting tar-like substance pooled on the floor, moved across the room and under the door.

Its voice echoed in Joe's head as he ran after it. 'There's that anger I was talking about...'

19

It was dusk when Campbell and Carpenter laid Raimi on the bench in the foyer. The storm clouds hid whatever sunset there might have been, and the natural light in the reception area was now fading.

'He's got a fever,' said Gladwin, feeling Raimi's forehead. She removed her suit jacket and placed it under his head. His eyes flickered left and right underneath their lids.

Wilson and Crompton emerged from the doors behind the reception. Wilson walked over to the bench where Raimi lay. 'What happened to him?'

Campbell swallowed. 'Don't know, guv. We found him in the steam-room.'

'What are all those scratches on his face and chest?'

'I don't know, guv. We found him like that.' Campbell rubbed his elbow, which still throbbed.

Wilson noticed his action. 'And what happened to you?'

'I slipped, guv. Fell on my elbow. I think I might have cracked the bone.'

'You slipped?'

Carpenter stepped in. 'It's true, guv. The whole locker room floor was covered in ice.'

Crompton now approached and placed his hand on Wilson's shoulder. 'We saw a lot of ice built up around the air vents down in the basement, didn't we, Wilson?'

Campbell took a deep breath, about to speak, but then changed his mind.

'Do you have something to add, officer?' said Wilson.

Campbell looked nervous. He looked away from his superior before he spoke. 'I'm scared, guv.'

'Scared? A big lad like you?'

'I'm starting to think Costello's story might be true, guv.' He looked at the floor when he spoke.

Wilson opened his mouth to speak, but Linda beat him to it. 'What story? What did Joseph tell you?' She stood up purposefully. 'What did he tell you, Francis? What happened on that camping trip?'

Wilson winced at the sound of his Christian name. 'It's Detective Wilson, Miss Williams. And you can ask him yourself in a minute.' He signalled to Campbell. 'Campbell, pull yourself together and come with me.'

Campbell and Wilson left reception and headed towards the interview rooms.

Crompton walked back around the reception desk and exited through the doors to the staff areas. He emerged moments later carrying a damp dishcloth from the kitchenette. He knelt down next to Gladwin and placed the cloth on Raimi's forehead. 'This should help,' he said, smiling.

Gladwin smiled back. 'Thank you, Sergeant.'

Linda sat back down after Wilson had left and turned to Curtis. 'What is going on? Stacey, please tell me.'

Curtis shrugged and placed her arm around Linda. 'I wish I knew.'

As soon as Wilson and Campbell stepped

into the corridor they were hit by a smell of blood. Campbell pulled his torch from his belt and shone it down the corridor. A trail of dried blood ran from interview room two to the stationary cupboard. 'I really don't like this, guv. Something isn't right here.' His heart was racing now and his torch light flittered from wall to wall as his hand trembled.

'Well, let's hope Costello can get the power back on and hopefully things will get back to normal.'

Campbell fumbled with the keys and unlocked the door to interview room three.

Wilson opened the door and shouted. 'Right, Costello —'

The emptiness of the room shut him up.

Campbell shone the torch round the room; the light caught on an upturned chair and then glistened from the shards of glass that were scattered across the floor. Blood pooled round the glass and splatter patterns spread up the wall underneath the hole where the mirror had once been.

They walked over to the gap in the wall, treading carefully. Peering through, they could see the trail of blood had begun on the other side and led towards the door of interview room two.

Exiting the room, they followed the trail to the stationery cupboard, expecting Joseph Costello to be on the other side. But he wasn't.

Panicking slightly, the officers turned to see a figure hobbling down the stairs. It burst through the fire exit, crashing into Wilson.

It was Joe. There was panic in his eyes as he blurted, 'We need to leave — NOW!'

20

Joe burst into the foyer with selfish purpose. Wilson was calling him back, and Campbell was lagging behind like a lost puppy dog.

'Costello! Get back here. I need to speak with you, now!' Wilson growled.

Joe didn't reply. He continued to march through the foyer, an arm tightly gripped across his belly. The commotion caused everyone (except for Raimi, who was still lying, semiconscious, on the bench) to stand to attention. Linda squealed in excitement to see her fiancé. She ran over to him, but he did not greet her. He gripped her by the wrist and dragged her towards the door. The blood-soaked shirt and his change in character scared her.

'Joseph, you're hurting my arm, baby,' said Linda, grimacing as his fingers tightened around her wrist, inflicting an unintentional Chinese burn.

'We're getting out of here,' he replied, still pulling her arm. He stopped at the automatic door, expecting it to open instantly. It did not. He waved his other hand in front of it. The doors remained closed.

'The doors aren't working, Costello,' called Wilson.

Joe ignored him. Instead, he proceeded to kick the door. 'C'mon — open, goddammit!'

He continued kicking at the door — three, four,

five times — but all this did was cause the glass to rattle in its frame.

'Joseph, stop it,' Linda pleaded. 'You're going to hurt yourself.'

Joe kicked again, six, seven times — then he screamed.

Linda gently placed her hand over his bicep and whispered, 'Joseph, we're stuck in here.'

'Power's out, Costello,' said Wilson, approaching. 'The doors are electric, and in case you haven't noticed we have no electricity. We're trapped in here for the night.'

Joe glared at him, his eyes wild. 'Then we're all dead.'

Raimi began to cough, turning Joe's attention away from Wilson.

Joe let go of Linda's arm (which she instantly rubbed, holding back tears) and marched over to the injured police officer. Raimi coughed again and convulsed.

'How long has he been like this?' Joe pointed to the wounds on Raimi's chest.

'Not sure,' said Carpenter. 'Campbell and I found him out cold in the steam-room.'

Gladwin still held her jacket under Raimi's head and Crompton still mopped his brow. 'Lad's got a really high fever,' Crompton observed.

The colour ran from Joe's face and he started to edge away from the bench. Curtis caught the look in Joe's face and stepped away. Carpenter did the same. They were unsure why, but something told the two officers it was a good idea.

Raimi coughed, even more violently, shooting black phlegm into Gladwin's face. The shock caused her to fall backward. She wiped the fluid from her face and inspected the oily substance that had collected on her fingertips. Raimi's entire body began to convulse, his arms and legs flailing. Crompton spread his weight over the officer's body in an attempt to restrain him. Raimi's eyes opened wide, and they were completely black.

Everyone watched in horror as Raimi spontaneously combusted.

Flames erupted into Crompton's face. He screamed, his hands reaching up to his cheeks. The sleeves of his shirt caught fire.

Carpenter and Curtis ran to the far side of the room, where a fire extinguisher and fire blanket were mounted on the wall. Carpenter took the blanket and wrapped it around Crompton, smothering the flames that had now burned through his shirt. Curtis worked the fire extinguisher, running over to Raimi's burning body as she fumbled with the pin. But the flames were already dying as she approached. All that remained of Benjamin Raimi was a scorch mark on the bench.

'Get back!' Joe ordered Curtis.

Like a jet-black phoenix, a Shadowman rose from the ashes of Raimi. It screamed, and everyone except Joe covered their ears, doubling over. The Shadowman reached out its icy hand and gripped Curtis by her throat, its frosty fingers nipping at her brown skin as it lifted her off the ground.

Wilson looked at Joe helplessly. 'Costello, is this one of those...?'

Joe nodded, stepping back to shield Linda. 'Everyone get back. Don't touch it.'

Gladwin inched away towards Wilson. Campbell crouched down next to Carpenter, who was nursing Crompton.

'You have to help her,' Linda whispered.

The Shadowman screamed again, this time in short, sharp shrieks. It was calling for help. Then it threw Curtis across the room. She landed on the reception desk, pulling the computer and telephone with her as she slid and fell down the other side. The Shadowman then turned to Gladwin and glided towards her.

Something caught Joe's eye and, with the Shadowman facing away from him, he sidestepped towards Officer Carpenter.

'Joe, don't leave me,' whimpered Linda.

The creature, sensing Linda was now exposed, turned its sights on her, shrieking once more.

Joe crouched down next to Carpenter and, without a word, pulled the police officer's torch from his belt.

The Shadowman launched itself towards Linda, its arms outstretched. It was stopped by a sharp whistle, like someone calling a dog. It turned to the source of the sound. Joe stood there, glaring, lip curled, the torch gripped with both hands. 'Let's go!'

He pushed the 'on' button and a bright beam of light shot from the torch. The Shadowman screeched, this time in pain, and a light frost spread on the floor beneath it as the nauseating smell of sulphur filled the room.

Joe charged at the Shadowman, swinging the torch. The creature shifted left, then right, dodging the beam. A third swing and the light caught the top of its head, which whitened and crumbled away. The thing screamed and reached out to claw at Joe, who swung the torch again. This time the light cut through the Shadowman's arm. The severed limb stiffened as it fell and exploded when it hit the floor. Joe lunged forward, aiming the torch at the Shadowman's chest. The blackness of the shadow faded to grey and its form began to crack and crumble before exploding into a cloud of ash.

Joe stood very still as the ash cloud settled. He was shaking; his heart was racing and adrenaline was pumping furiously around his body. When he regained his senses, he threw the torch back to Carpenter and pulled Linda towards him. He wrapped his arms round her, burying his head into her shoulder. Something inside him broke and he began to cry.

21

The foyer was now in darkness, except for the occasional flash of lightning as the storm passed overhead, illuminating the room with a strobe effect.

After Joe had composed himself, he brought everyone up to speed with the events of his stag do and what he had learned about the Shadowmen during his time in Druid Wood. Yet, for reasons unknown to him — embarrassment or shame, maybe — he kept the encounter with the doppelganger to himself. And, following the recent commotion, everyone in the room had either forgotten or not noticed his wounded stomach.

Wilson made a further telephone call to the commissioner's office. When the call ended, he threw his mobile phone at the wall and then kicked the reception desk several times.

What remained of the Raven's Peak police force sat morosely huddled in the station's reception. The smell of sulphur still lingered. Curtis nursed the bruises to her head with an ice-pack from the reception's first-aid kit. Crompton sat with his hands bandaged and gauze fixed to his face from the same kit. Campbell had the light of his torch aimed at the doorway that led to the interview rooms and beyond, while Carpenter pointed his at the area behind the reception desk (after being advised to do so by Joe).

Gladwin approached Wilson, picked up his phone and handed it back to him. The screen was cracked and the back would no longer stay fixed in place, but it still functioned. 'Bad news, I take it?' she asked.

Wilson snatched the phone from her, and then succumbed to a coughing fit. Once he had caught his breath, he replied. 'No one is coming out until the morning,' he said, keeping his voice low.

'Okay. So what do we do now? I really don't think you're prepared to sit and wait.'

'Damn right I'm not.' Wilson turned to Joe just as another flash of lightning briefly lit up the room.

Linda, who had been dozing with her head resting on her fiancé's shoulder, jumped upright as thunder boomed overhead.

'Costello, do you think you could get the power back on in here?' Wilson asked.

Joe shrugged. 'I don't know. Maybe.'

'Well, it won't do any harm to take a look, will it?'

Joe sighed and stood up. Linda gripped his arm, looking up at him with panic in her eyes. He smiled. 'I won't be long. You'll be okay here. Just make sure you stay close to someone with a torch.'

Curtis unfastened her torch from her belt and handed it to Linda. 'You can use mine if it helps.'

'Thank you,' she said, taking the torch.

'Crompton, give Costello yours,' Wilson ordered.

Crompton obeyed without saying a word and handed Joe his torch.

Wilson then turned to Gladwin. 'You'd better

bring those two from the lock-up in here. Take Carpenter with you.'

Gladwin nodded. 'Yes, guv.'

Campbell now stood. 'What about me, guv?'

'You, Mr Broken Elbow, can keep an eye on things in here while we're gone. D'you think you can handle that?'

Campbell nodded. 'Yes, sir!'

Joe and Wilson made their way down to the basement. As they walked, Wilson questioned him further about the night in the woods. This time, between the coughing fits, there was actually empathy and sincerity in his voice. No matter how many times he told it, Joe's story remained the same.

'So, do you think Mikey is one of those things now? Christ, I sound like a lunatic just for asking that question.'

Joe had known the Wilsons since childhood, but, with the exception of Mike, they had never warmed to him or Tony. He had never really known why; even Mike was unable to provide a real answer. But the closest he could figure was that Mrs Wilson was a strong, traditional woman and she didn't like her baby boy associating with someone with foreign blood — especially someone whose father (who had a reputation for being a crook) would leave a mother with two young boys. Maybe she feared Joe had inherited his father's attributes and this would rub off on her youngest son — an attitude that had undoubtedly been passed to her eldest. As such, Joe had always kept his guard up around Francis Patrick Wilson.

'I guess so,' Joe answered, avoiding eye contact.

'And your brother, too?'

Joe bit his lip. 'Yeah.'

'But you don't know for certain. They could still be out in the woods somewhere, couldn't they?'

'Possibly...' Joe sighed. 'But I doubt it.' He now looked at Wilson for a moment. 'I mean, I hoped they *would* be out there somewhere.' He shook his head. 'But now, I'm not so sure.'

'You've changed your mind pretty quick, Costello. Is there something you're not telling me?'

Joe contemplated confessing about the entity he had bled from his stomach, his dark doppelganger, a Shadowman evolved, but he still kept this to himself. Besides, he had not seen the thing since. Perhaps it had perished without a host.

He shrugged again. 'I just mean, after what happened back there, I'm starting to...' He paused, looking for words. 'I'm starting to lose faith.'

* * *

Barons' wait was now over as his cellmate began to combust. It had taken longer than anticipated; the old drunkard must have had some fight left in him, after all. But now, as the flames died, all that remained of him was a scorch mark burned into the mattress.

From the ash a Shadowman rose. It screamed at Barons as frost crystallised on the cell bars. It lunged towards him, wrapping its fingers around his neck. Then, sensing something behind the icy-blue eyes of this frail man, it let go, edged backwards and disappeared into the darkness.

Barons smiled to himself, then, hearing the cell-block doors open, sat on the floor in the corner of the cell.

* * *

'I can't fix this,' said Joe, shaking his head.

'What do you mean you can't fix it?' said Wilson, before having another violent coughing fit. His hand was still cupped as he moved it away from his mouth, and he glanced at the blood he had spat onto his palm before discreetly wiping the stain on the back of his trousers.

Joe cast him a concerned look, but Wilson's eyes told him not to pry. Joe cast the light of his torch over the damaged fuse boxes and tattered wiring. 'These are completely wrecked, look. This can't be fixed; each unit needs replacing.'

Wilson looked up at the ceiling, placed his hands on his hips and swore under his breath. He stood for a moment, silent except for the clicking of his tongue against the roof of his mouth. He stared at the damaged fuse boxes, willing them to fix themselves. 'D'you think your Shadowmen did this?'

Joe shrugged. 'Maybe. Who knows?'

Wilson's eyes lit up. 'I think I know someone who knows. C'mon.' He turned and left the storeroom.

Joe followed.

From the air vents above, droplets of thick black liquid fell, forming a sticky pool of tar on the concrete floor. Once the puddle was three feet in diameter, it began to ooze forwards in a serpentine motion and seeped under the door, creeping silently behind Joe and Wilson.

22

'Oh my God! Oh my God!' Barons sat in the corner of the cell rocking back and forth as Gladwin and Carpenter entered. His knees were clutched against his chest and his long, straggly, straw-like hair was covering his face. 'Oh God, don't let it hurt me! Oh God!'

Carpenter fumbled the lock of the cell door as he tried to work the keys with the same hand in which he held his torch. Gladwin scanned the cell. 'Where's Davey?' she asked.

The lock clicked and Carpenter pulled the door open; it screeched as the rusted hinges ground against each other. He searched the cell with the torchlight and saw the scorch marks on the bed. 'Gladwin — look.'

Gladwin turned her head to the bed then crouched in front of Barons. 'What happened? Where's the man who was in here with you?'

'Oh God! Oh God!' Barons continued to rock back and forth.

'Mr Barons, can you tell me what happened?'

'Oh God, don't let them take me.'

'Barons, come on. Pull yourself together!'

'Oh God, Oh G —'

Gladwin smacked Barons across the cheek. The slap made Carpenter flinch with an empathetic sting.

Barons stared at Gladwin in stunned silence,

his hands shaking.

'What happened?' she asked again.

'H-h-he j-just burst, burst into flames. Oh God!'

Carpenter crouched next to Gladwin and whispered, 'Just like Raimi.'

Gladwin ignored him, focusing on Barons. 'Then what happened?' The tone of her voice was now lower, more soothing.

Barons sniffled. 'Wh-what was left of him… God, what was left turned into a-a-a…'

'Go on. A what?'

'A demon!'

* * *

Officer Campbell awoke to find himself in a heap on the foyer floor, his fingers wrapped round his torch. His neck ached, his head throbbed and there were deep scratches on his face and the back of his hands. He tried to pull himself up onto one of the benches, but the pain in his elbow worsened and white heat surged through his arm, making him whimper. As he lifted himself, his feet slipped out from underneath him on one of the icy patches that now scattered the reception area. The windows and the glass of the automatic doors were frosted and the smell of rotten eggs was stronger than before.

It was not until he had finally sat on the bench that Campbell realised how silent the reception room now was; the only sound he could hear was his own breath. He shone the torch across the room illuminating the opposite benches, the posters on noticeboard, the fire extinguisher mounted to the far wall, the scorched fragments of the fire-blanket that had once covered Sergeant Crompton, the wrecked reception desk and several smashed torches that lay scattered on the floor.

He sat alone, shaking from a combination of cold and shock.

* * *

Wilson coughed and coughed, his upper body convulsing. He doubled over, barking, one hand covering his mouth, the other clutching his chest. 'If we make it out of here, you need to get that checked out,' said Joe.

'Like you care,' wheezed Wilson.

Joe laughed. 'Just because we don't get on doesn't mean I don't care.'

Wilson coughed again, this time more violently. A glob of blood shot up from his throat and splattered on the floor. Over the sound of the coughing and in the failed light, Joe didn't notice the extent of Wilson's ailment.

The detective composed himself and stood up straight, clearing his throat. 'Let's keep moving.'

The tar puddle continued to meander in pursuit until it came across the small pool of blood that Wilson had coughed up. It paused for moment, then oozed over the red fluid, absorbing it into itself. It then began to bubble and expand. Once the blood had been fully absorbed, it moved on. The floor tiles began to crack and perish as it passed over them.

Wilson keeled over again, coughing. Joe helped him to his feet. 'Jesus, Francis. You are clearly not well.'

Wilson pushed him away. 'I'm fine — and it's

none of your concern,' he growled. That rapport that had begun to build between them was now gone. 'You go on. I just want a minute to catch my breath.'

'I don't think so. You can barely stand.'

The detective pushed him again. 'Just go!' he cried. 'Tell Gladwin to bring Barons to my office. I have a —' He began coughing again. 'I have a few questions for him.'

'What's his story, anyway?'

'Just go!'

Joe clenched his fists and sighed. 'Alright.' He turned and left the corridor through the nearest exit, reluctantly leaving Wilson on his own.

23

Campbell's teeth clashed violently together as the blow connected with the underside of his jaw, reverberating through his skull. He staggered back, clutching the wall, his mouth filling with blood. Joe came at him again, taking another swing, but before his fist could connect his arm was yanked back by Gladwin.

'That's enough!' she shouted.

Joe backed off, but rage still flooded through him.

Gladwin glared up at him. 'You know I should arrest you for striking a police officer.'

Campbell straightened up. 'It's okay, ma'am. I won't press charges.' He rubbed his chin whilst repeatedly clenching his jaw. 'I should have been...' He dropped his gaze down to his feet and mumbled, 'looking out for them.'

Baron, who was handcuffed, stepped forward, breaking the atmosphere. 'Did the demons take them?'

'Demons?' Joe turned to look at the prisoner. 'You mean the shadows?'

Campbell now rubbed the back of his neck. 'Yes. Demons, Shadowmen, whatever you want to call them. They took Curtis and your fiancée, Joe.'

'*Demons?*' Joe repeated.

'Yes, that's what they are,' said Barons.

Carpenter scoffed. 'You're sure of that, are you?'

'Oh yes, quite sure.' Barons nodded, but his eyes were on Joe, staring at the bloodstains that were soaked into the bottom of his shirt. 'What happened to you?' Looking at Joe caused alarm bells to ring in his head. He didn't know what it was, but something sent the dark entity hiding inside him into frenzy.

Similarly, there was something in Barons' eyes that set Joe on edge.

'Mr Barons,' Gladwin said, saving Joe from having to answer, 'whatever it is we are dealing with here, you seem to know a lot about it. Maybe you can fill everyone in when we regroup with Detective Wilson…'

* * *

Minutes later, they were in Wilson's office waiting for the man himself to arrive. With the exception of feet tapping on the floor, fingers drumming on the desk and the occasional sigh, there was silence.

Campbell's jaw clicked, disturbing the atmosphere. 'Quite a left hook you got there, Costello. D'you box?'

'Uh… sorry about that,' said Joe, looking at his hands. 'I just want to find Linda and get out of here. And yeah, my dad showed me a few moves. Before he left, that is.'

'We'll find them,' said Gladwin. 'Let's just wait for Wilson, and then Mr Barons can tell us what he knows. His information may help us find Miss Williams and Officer Curtis.'

The door opened and Wilson walked in slowly, dragging his heels. His complexion was pale, his eyes were bloodshot and his lips chapped.

'Jesus!' Carpenter exclaimed, staring at his superior in shock.

'Francis!' Gladwin put her arm around him and helped him to his chair. 'What happened to you?'

Wilson coughed. 'I'm alright, just tired. Where are Curtis and the future Mrs Costello?'

'Those things have taken them, guv,' said Campbell.

'Yeah,' Joe said, 'and we need to find them before...'

'Before what, Costello?' asked Wilson. 'Before they turn into one? After all, that's what you think happened to Mikey and your own brother, isn't it?'

Barons coughed to clear his throat. 'He is right. That is what will happen, sooner or later.'

'Ah, Mr Barons,' said Wilson. 'You've become garrulous all of a sudden. It wasn't so long ago that the only words you would say were "no comment".'

'Well, yes. That was before I realised the extent of the situation,' answered Barons.

Wilson rolled his eyes. 'Then perhaps you should fill us in.'

'Yes, of course...' said Barons. 'Whether you believe or not, these creatures — these *shadows* — are demons, for want of a better word. They were once human, of course, but their souls were tortured and twisted by another demon feeding from it, stealing its energy and the person's humanity until all that remains is darkness. After all, isn't darkness only the absence of light?'

'But these demons hate the light. It hurts

them — it even kills them,' said Joe, offering his own insight.

'It is not the light itself that they are afraid of, it is what it represents,' Barons argued.

'And what exactly does it represent?' asked Wilson, struggling to get the words out through another bout of coughing.

Barons smiled. 'Light is hope. It is the good and the divine. It brings life. It is everything that these demons are not.'

'And how do you know so much about this?' Gladwin asked.

'Yeah, and why were you skulking around Druid Wood?' added Carpenter. 'And what's with that old knife we found on you and your tattoos?'

Barons shrugged. 'I have spent most of my life studying demonology and other worldly dimensions. The marks on my arms are not merely tattoos. They are passages of ancient text that you would simply not understand. I'm ashamed to say that I ran into a few financial difficulties and my debtor began to take an interest in my work. He thought a demon would grant him fortune and power. He said if I resurrected a demon that could grant such a wish, he would write off all my debts.' He paused, looking wistful. 'It was something I had never tried before, although I'd always contemplated it. I was confident I had accurately translated the text and could summon a small, lesser demon. However, in order to do so a sacrifice had to be made —'

'A sacrifice?' interrupted Joe.

'Yes, an offering of blood. But the blood needed to be let using a special, ancient dagger like the one you took from me.'

'Only it didn't go to plan, did it?' said Joe.

'No, the demon wasn't quite what I expected. It couldn't be bargained with, and neither could it see reason; it just consumed everything it could — and more of its kind followed. They spoke in unison. They had no independent thought; instead they were a collective mind.'

Wilson stood up. 'So, let me get this straight… *You* summoned these things?'

Barons only nodded in response.

'Then it's reasonable to assume you can send them back to wherever they came from.'

'Back to their own dimension?' Barons said slowly. 'Yes… yes, I guess it's possible.' He looked up sharply. 'I will need the dagger to do that, though.'

'Gladwin, where's this dagger gone?' Wilson asked.

'I locked it away as evidence, sir.'

'Go get it,' ordered Wilson.

Joe was troubled. What this Barons had said seemed to fit in with what had happened that night in Druid Wood, but it didn't explain the thing that he had cut from his stomach. 'Doesn't make sense…' Joe mumbled to himself.

'You have another idea, Costello?' said Wilson, overhearing.

Everyone stared at him, but the stare from Barons was the most unsettling. 'What doesn't make sense?' he asked. 'I can assure you I'm speaking the truth. You never answered me earlier, when I asked what had happened to you.'

Joe felt very uncomfortable, and his cheeks suddenly flushed. Whatever it was that had escaped from him *was* him; if the people around him knew that fact, and saw that it was him, how would they react? How would *Linda* react?

'Yes, Costello,' said Wilson, who was now looking even paler and worse for wear. 'You never did tell me how you came to leave a trail of blood in my police station.'

Joe looked from Wilson to Barons. If he really could send these things back, back to where they came from, maybe his doppelganger would be sent back, too. And besides, his darker side hadn't been seen since the encounter in the upstairs offices.

'Are you sure you can send these things back?' Joe asked Barons.

'Yes, I'm certain.'

Joe licked his lips; his mouth had begun to dry rapidly with anticipation. 'I think there is something else in here with us,' he said shakily.

There was no response. The room remained silent. Either the survivors could not comprehend the possibility of there being something other than 'demons' lurking the corridors of Raven's Peak Police Station or they were too tired to care. After all, what else could be worse than 'demons'?

And so, without any protest from the others, Joe reluctantly began to explain why there was a row of staples in his stomach and concluded with his own observations of the thing that had been born from him. 'It's not like the others, though. This thing has more depth to it, more dimensions.' He shrugged. 'It's not a shadow. It spoke to me — we had an actual conversation. It wasn't speaking in time with the others, like back in the woods. This was a free entity, independent of the Shadowmen.'

Barons looked nervous; something inside him

told him he needed to be afraid of this new being. The word 'abomination' echoed through his mind. If anyone had noticed the fear in his eyes, given the situation they found themselves in, no one would have thought anything out of the ordinary about it.

'It said it had been feeding on my blood. It looked just like me,' Joe continued. 'I don't know, maybe it absorbed my DNA somehow. Inherited my genes. Maybe it takes on the form and abilities of its former host while it looks for a new one.' Joe buried his face in his hands. 'I need to find Linda.'

Gladwin spoke. 'Well, no one has seen this thing. I think we should proceed in assisting Mr Barons, and if we come across this other demon we'll deal with it. What do you think, guv?'

Wilson did not respond. Instead he sat slumped, eyes closed, in his desk chair.

24

'Wilson!' Gladwin gently shook her boss; there was no response. His head slumped forward, his chin resting on his chest. She placed two fingers on his neck, trying to find a pulse. There was none.

'Is he dead?' asked Carpenter.

'I don't know,' she replied, still trying to find a pulse. She moved her fingers closer towards Wilson's jaw. As she pushed her fingertips against the senior detective's neck the skin broke and Gladwin's fingers dipped deep into the tissue. She jumped back, yanking her fingers from the wound. Sticky black tar ran down the back of her hand. The substance began to consume her skin like flesh-eating bacteria and Gladwin screamed as she shook her gangrenous hand in an attempt to fling the substance from her. The liquid leapt from her hand and hit the desk, eating its way through the wood.

Gladwin gritted her teeth and wiped her hand on the back of her trousers. The pain was fading.

Everyone now backed up against the opposite wall, staring at Wilson. They watched as his skin began to blacken and crack, scabbing from head to toe. Dark liquid began to seep from the wounds and ate through Wilson's suit. The dead flesh began to fall away, revealing something that seemed to resemble Joe's mythical creature. Only now it was a dark duplicate of Wilson.

'The abomination,' whispered Barons.

The creature stood up and placed a hand against the nearest wall. Black tendrils oozed from its touch and spread across the masonry. As it did so paint began to crack and crumble, the plaster decaying and breaking away from the wall. The creature then placed its other hand on the top of the desk. More tendrils spread across the desk like vines of ebony ivy, and the wooden frame began to rot. The desk collapsed under the weight of the office equipment.

Gladwin brushed up against Joe, clutching his arm. 'Is this...?'

'Afraid so.'

Joe switched on his torch and shone it at the abomination. The creature's body began to smoulder where the light connected, but nothing more. It didn't explode like the Shadowmen had done. Instead it began to increase in mass. Its oily arm stretched out towards Joe. Droplets of tar ran from it and cascaded onto the floor, causing the wood of the laminate to decompose as it pooled. The creature pulled the torch from Joe's hand, not even fazed by the light. Its fingers wrapped around the torch, causing the glass in the lens to disintegrate. Grains of sand sprinkled to the floor and the rubber of the handle began to perish. Joe backed off, pulling Gladwin with him.

'Forget this,' grunted Carpenter, unclipping his torch from his belt. He shone the light directly into the thing's open mouth. The back of its head began to emit smoke as it screamed. The sound was more like a wheeze than a cry, like something too large for a vacuum cleaner had got lodged in the piping. The light slowly began to burn its way through the shadowy doppelganger's throat and then a ray of light burst from the back of its neck. The creature wailed and lashed out at Carpenter, knocking the torch out of his hand. It swung its hand back and gripped the young officer by the neck, its claws digging deep into his jugular.

Carpenter began to convulse as his skin rippled from his neck across his cheeks to his forehead in the wake of its tendrils burrowing underneath. His eyes rolled back in their sockets, a milky liquid seeped from the corner of his mouth and blood ran from his nose. The colour ran from his flesh as cysts and pox marks began to form and then blacken on his face. At the same time the policeman began to appear emaciated — it was like his insides were being turned to soup and sucked from him. This thing was feeding from him in the way a spider would feed from its prey, and as it did so it began to grow in mass and height. Joe could feel it watching him as it fed from the police officer, laughing at him, but all he could do was stand petrified with terror.

All that now remained of Carpenter was a blacked hide draped in a policeman's uniform. The creature discarded the husk, which exploded into a pool of black slop as it hit the floor. The sound shook Joe from his state of catatonia. He ran for the door, pulling Gladwin and Barons with him. Campbell came to from the sudden commotion and followed the others out as they fled the office, slamming the door shut behind him.

25

Linda awoke with a sharp breath. Her chest ached from the sudden intake of air. She lay for a moment on the cold floor, trying to regain her senses, but recent events escaped her memory. She sat up and attempted to look around the room. There was no light to see by but her ears picked up the sound of someone breathing next to her. She fumbled around until her fingertips touched the warmth of a human body. She felt for the face and began to gently slap the person's cheeks. 'Wake up,' she said. 'Please wake up!'

There was a faint groan and then she felt her hand being pushed away. 'Who's there?' croaked the person. The voice belonged to a young woman.

'Linda Williams.'

'Linda?' The woman began to sit up. 'It's Officer Curtis — Stacey.'

'Are you okay, officer?'

Curtis coughed to clear her throat. 'Yes, I think so. And I think given the circumstances you can just call me Stacey. Where are we?'

Linda shrugged then realised Curtis probably couldn't see her body language. 'I don't know,' she replied. 'But I think we are still in the police station.'

'Is there anyone else in here with us?'

'No, I don't think so,' replied Linda.

'Help me up,' said Curtis, her tone now more assertive.

Linda fumbled around until she had a firm grip on Curtis' arm and together they stood up. Curtis stretched her arms out in front and cautiously stepped forward. After a few paces her hands touched a metallic object. She ran her fingers around it and found it seemed to stretch up from the floor. Her fingers then fell upon a wooden texture that shot off at a right angle to the metal. She followed the wood, which was smooth and polished to touch, until her fingertips reached what felt like cardboard. Inside the box she could feel wads of paper. 'I think we're in one of the old filing rooms,' she said.

She ran her fingers back the other direction away from the shelf and onto the wall. After fumbling further along, she touched the light switch. Hoping by some miracle the power was back on, she flipped the switch. Nothing.

Her fingers now found the door and she reached down to the handle. She jolted her hand back as the cold of the handle nipped at her hand.

Linda sensed her flinch. 'What's wrong?'

'It's ice cold. Frozen, in fact.'

Curtis tried the handle again; she could feel her palm sticking to the metal as icy pains shot through her arm. She pulled at the handle the best she could, but it wouldn't budge.

Linda didn't have to be told they were stuck here; in her heart she knew what the situation was. She said a silent prayer. *Joe, where are you?*

26

Gladwin led the troop to the evidence room, not stopping until they reached it. The creature that had materialised from the late Detective Wilson's body could be heard screaming somewhere, its cries echoing around the building. During the dash to the evidence room they had encountered several Shadowmen. They had been dispatched easily enough and Gladwin was beginning to believe they may have been able to make it through the night if it hadn't been for this new being. The light from Carpenter's torch had barely done any damage, except...

Gladwin turned to Joe. 'The light didn't do anything to it,' she said, 'except when Carpenter shone his torch directly into its mouth. Did you notice?'

Joe nodded. 'Yeah. When the light shone on its exterior — nothing. But...' He paused, gathering his thoughts. 'But when the light got inside it... Well, it didn't like that.'

'Maybe we could use that against it somehow.' Then she cried out in frustration. 'I don't know what I'm supposed to do!'

Joe placed a hand on her shoulder. 'Hopefully this Barons fellow can send it back to wherever it came from,' he said, and she looked up at him with a rare smile. 'Let's just try to not let anyone else die,' he added, nudging her with his elbow.

'I've found it, ma'am!' Campbell called from behind one of the cabinets, waving the blade above his head. It was still in an evidence bag.

Barons rushed over to him, trying to snatch the blade out of his hands. 'Be careful with that — it's hundreds of years old.'

Campbell held the blade out of reach and looked at Gladwin for orders. 'Ma'am?'

'Mr Barons,' said Gladwin, 'I'm about to allow you to take possession of an offensive weapon. I'll be watching you closely.'

'I understand,' said Barons.

Campbell handed him the blade and he clenched it tightly to his chest as if protecting a child.

'Oh, and Mr Barons,' Gladwin continued, 'if you try anything funny I will feed you to that thing out there. Understood?'

Joe was taken back and Campbell sniggered at the detective's fighting talk.

'So what happens now?' asked Campbell.

'The ritual is quite simple, really,' said Barons, not taking his eye off the engravings on the blade. 'I'm effectively going to open a doorway to another dimension, like a vortex, and it will draw all these demons in. Once they are all returned the doorway should close.'

'*Should* close?' said Joe.

Barons looked up. 'In theory.'

'Great… well, I will leave you three to it,' Joe said as he turned to leave the evidence room.

'Where are you going?' Gladwin pulled him back.

'I'm going to find my fiancée.'

'Do you think she is still alive, with that thing out there?'

'I have to hope so.'

Gladwin sighed. 'Okay, I can't stop you I suppose. Just be careful.'

'I will. Wait, what's in there?' Joe was distracted by a door at the far end of the room. What caught his attention was the bright yellow sign with a black lightning bolt running through the middle of it.

'Nothing really.' Gladwin was puzzled. 'It's just where we keep electrical equipment. Light bulbs, computer cables, that sort of thing. Why do you ask?'

Joe smirked then licked his lips. 'Because maybe I can show these things the light.'

* * *

The abomination, as Barons had called it, had oozed out of Wilson's office and once into the foyer it returned to the humanoid shape of Wilson. The black tendrils continued to spread from its hands as it touched the walls, causing the paint and plaster to decay. The laminate flooring began to dampen and rot as the creature walked over it. As it made its way through the corridors of the police station decay began to spread like a cancer, consuming everything in its path. The creature skulked down to the holding cells, the metal doors rusting as it ran its hands along them. And then it came face to face with a Shadowman.

The Shadowman held its position, its head bobbing up and down, trying to make sense of this thing in front of it; its collective consciousness had not encountered anything like this before, yet there was a sense of familiarity about it. It edged forward slightly and then came its orders from the collective. The Shadowman howled and lunged at the creature.

The creature did not back away. It stood its ground, catching the Shadowman in its arms. The Shadowman wriggled and squirmed, trying to break free from the creature's grip to no avail. Instead it found itself being absorbed into the creature — consumed — until nothing of it remained.

The abomination, Wilson's doppelganger, roared and began to increase in size, as it had done when feeding from Carpenter. Then it continued on its way, looking for more to consume.

27

With one swift swoop of his arm Joe cleared a shelf. Boxes and other bits and pieces fell to the floor with a clatter. A set of step-ladders sat in the corner. The metal legs crashed together as he carried them to the centre of the room. The ladder rattled as a heavy foot landed on each rung.

Joe reached up and twisted the fluorescent tubing. The bulb screeched with each turn as it was loosened from its fitting. Next he tore off a length of duct tape with his teeth and wrapped it around several nine-volt batteries, keeping them bunched together. He then cut the plug from a computer power cable and sliced the opposite end, which would have normally fitted in the base unit; the wire cutters glided through the copper with two snips.

He repeated the action with a second power cable. *Snip-snip.*

Joe then cut away the protective sheaf at both ends of each piece of cable to expose the copper wiring. Using more duct tape, he held the battery pack to his waist, wrapping it round several times for good measure. He connected one end of each cable to the ends of the fluorescent tubing — the loose end of each wire connected to the batteries. He held the bulb in both hands like a sword and it began to buzz and flicker. Finally, it stopped blinking and steadied. The glow was faint at first but quickly grew brighter until it was almost unbearable to look at directly.

Joe winked at Gladwin. 'I'm not just a pretty face.'

Barons had explained that in order to perform the ritual he would need somewhere with plenty of space and exposure to the moonlight. So, Gladwin gave Campbell her keys and told him to lead Barons to the rooftop. The officer obliged and led Barons to the stairwell.

'You not going with them?' Joe asked.

'No,' she said, 'I'm coming with you.'

'No chance,' Joe protested. 'I have no idea what is out there, especially with that other thing on the loose. Besides, I don't trust Barons. It's his fault we're in this mess. He let them all loose to begin with.'

'And he's going to send them all back. Campbell won't let him try any funny business.'

Joe shook his head. 'Look, I appreciate your help, but —'

'I'm not helping you. I'm going to look for Curtis. I can't leave her behind, not without knowing whether she is alive or not.'

Joe sighed. 'You sound like someone I thought I once knew.' There was a moment's silence and then he said, 'Alright, but you're going to need fresh batteries in that torch.'

After changing the batteries, Joe and Gladwin stepped out into the foyer. The smell hit them first before they saw the desolation: a miasma of rotten flesh, damp and stale tobacco rolled into one. Joe screwed up his nose. Gladwin felt the reflux of digestive acids burn her oesophagus as she clapped her free hand across her mouth.

Once the initial shock of the smell had passed, they shone their lights around the foyer, observing the crumbling walls, the rotten floor boards and the rusted metals. It was like something had eaten away at the building, like maggots devouring flesh until all that remained was the bone.

Trailing across what remained of the foyer were traces of black liquid leading behind the reception. Joe moved the fluorescent tubing nearer to it, and as he did the substance began to sizzle and then dry until it crumbled into ash. The pair followed the trail, taking slow, steady steps; their footfalls echoed eerily in the silence of the room.

Joe's heart raced as they descended the steps to the holding cells, his pulse throbbing in his wrists and neck. His hand began to shake and he gripped the fluorescent tube tighter. He wanted to breathe heavily but instead held his breath, staggering the exhale in the hope that Gladwin wouldn't notice he was afraid. But as they followed the trail she moved closer and closer to him until, without even releasing it, she was now holding tightly to his arm.

There was something else they had failed to notice… since beginning their search for Linda and Curtis, they hadn't encountered a single Shadowman.

* * *

Using the blade, Barons began to scratch a circle, about ten feet in diameter, into the floor. The open sky above began to rumble and the storm clouds finally burst.

'Great, that's all we need,' said Campbell, looking up at a black, starless sky.

Barons didn't respond; he continued his work, muttering to himself, as he received the instructions from a voice within. He started to scratch symbols within the circle. Campbell noticed they looked similar to the tattoos on Barons' arms, and he moved to the edge of the circle for a better look. Being careful not to actually step into the circle, he warily leant his upper body over the line as Barons appeared to have finished.

'So, what happens now?' Campbell asked gingerly.

Barons stepped back to stand next to the big police officer. 'Now,' he said, not taking his eyes off his handiwork, 'we need a sacrifice.'

'A sacrifice?'

But before Campbell's mind could connect the dots he felt a sudden coldness. He choked and spluttered as the ancient blade severed his jugular. Barons pulled the blade back and Campbell dropped to his knees, clutching at his neck, the warm blood pumping between his fingers. His entire body felt frozen and he began to shiver as dizziness overcame him. Gagging on the blood that filled his throat, he fell face down into the centre of the circle. The blood now gushed from the wound and flowed into the grooves of the scratches.

Barons sneered and began chuckling to himself. The sound grew louder and turned into uncontrollable laughter.

* * *

'What was that?' Linda asked, running to the back of the storeroom as a cry echoed from the other side of the door.

'I don't know,' said Curtis, slowly backing away from the door. 'One of those things, probably.'

Linda shook her head. 'Maybe, but that sounded different.' She shivered as a draught began to blow from under the door and then she coughed as the smell of sulphur flowed through her nose and into her lungs.

Two Shadowmen materialised from under the door. Although the two women could not see them they could sense they were there, and they cowered in the corner of the room.

Icy fingers wrapped round Curtis' ankle and began to pull her forward. She reached out and flung her arms around the frame of one of the shelves, but the pull of the Shadowman was too strong and her grip was quickly broken. She then felt the cold pass over her legs, cross her stomach and reach her chest. The claws of the Shadowman tore through her clothing and buried deep into her breasts. As the cold spread through her body she slowly began to drift out of consciousness.

The other Shadowman pulled at Linda and she fell face down as it dragged her closer, her fingernails scrabbling to find purchase on the floor. The Shadowman then plunged its sharp fingers into her back, just below the shoulder blades. Linda's entire back arched in agony, but the pain soon subsided as the cold set in.

With a screech of grinding metal, the storeroom door was torn away from its hinges and flung down the corridor. Towering in the doorway was Wilson's doppelganger. It roared a deep, phlegm-filled growl and then reached into the room to grab the Shadowman that was feeding on Curtis. The Shadowman lashed out its long, spindly limbs as it was lifted by its head, but to no avail.

The abomination opened its mouth wide, its jaws like a snake's, and a long black tongue lashed left and right. It lifted the Shadowman above its head and then dropped the demon into its mouth, its jaws snapping shut afterwards. Black drool splattered against the wall with a sizzling hiss.

With a shriek, the remaining Shadowman abandoned Linda and darted out of the storeroom. The abomination spun round and caught it with one hand, pinning it to the wall. The Shadowman squealed and squirmed as those snake-like jaws engulfed it whole.

But a diet of tortured souls did little to sustain this new species. It wanted flesh and blood. And it now turned its sights on the two women who lay semi-conscious on the storeroom floor.

28

The creature lurched in the storeroom doorway, its tongue flitting in and out of its toothless mouth. Its breath was gravelly, exhaling in short, sharp bursts, almost as if the thing was sniggering to itself.

It reached a black, greasy arm into the room and took hold of Curtis' leg. The tar-like fluids from its hand ate through the fabric of her trousers and gnawed the skin underneath. The pain caused her to stir from her semi-conscious state. She screamed as her eyes focused on the thing that had hold of her and then she cried out again as the substance oozing from the thing's hands burrowed deeper into her calf muscle.

The creature reached in with its other hand and took hold of Curtis with an overhand grip across her shoulder. Its thumb dug through her shirt and into the flesh of her left breast while its fingers wormed deep into her back. As with her former partner, her skin began to ripple as something squirmed within. Marks began to blister on her face and then the skin cracked and blackened. Her entire body was consumed with the most extreme pain she had ever felt, as if every single bone in her body had shattered simultaneously while her insides began to boil. As she passed out the last thing she heard was a sharp whistle.

* * *

The monster turned in the direction of the sound. Stood at the far end of the corridor was Joe wielding the fluorescent tube, which glowed brightly. Gladwin stood behind him, armed with her torch as if she were holding a hand gun.

'Let's do this!' Joe bellowed.

'Costello!' Wilson's doppelganger growled.

It dropped Curtis and charged along the corridor towards Joe and Gladwin. At about half of the distance it stopped and slammed its palms down on the floor. Those black tendrils spun from its fingers and spread across the floor and walls, causing destruction in their wake.

Joe jumped back, pushing Gladwin with him as the blackness came to a halt at the spot he had been standing. The tip of his boot scraped against the substance, which ate through the leather. Gladwin shone her torch at the webbing and it disintegrated.

Another wave of black decay spread down the corridor towards Gladwin; more paint and plaster crumbled from the walls. Acting quickly, her heart beating rapidly, Gladwin's training kicked in and she swiftly picked off the substance with the light of her torch.

Wilson's doppelganger let out a roar of disappointment. Joe and Gladwin looked at each other, their eyes wide, sweat dripping from their brows. They nodded grimly and charged. Joe led, wielding his 'sword', Gladwin ready to take out whatever was thrown at them.

It swung a club-like fist at Joe, who spun on his heel, dodging the blow, and countered it with the fluorescent tubing. The weapon cut through the creature's arm like a surgical laser and the severed limb dropped to the floor. Detached from the body, it liquefied, collecting into a puddle of tar. The ooze began to flow back towards its owner, but before it had a chance to reconnect Gladwin hit it with the torchlight.

The other fist came at Joe. Reacting quickly, he made a backhanded swing with the tubing and severed the creature's other arm. Joe licked his lips and shook with both fear and adrenalin. He then swept low at the legs, cutting them both from the body.

Slumped on its knees, the head and torso of Wilson's doppelganger roared and lashed its lizard-like tongue at Joe. It wrapped around the fluorescent tubing and, although the light was obviously burning it, the tongue did not loosen its grip. Joe, taken back, lost his grip on the tube. The creature yanked its head back and pulled the weapon out of Joe's hands, snapping the wiring from the batteries. Joe lost his balance and fell back as the creature smashed the tubing against the wall.

It morphed into a Shadowman-like form and then dropped onto its front, slithering towards Joe, its tongue lashing left and right. Joe tried to pull himself up but his feet kept slipping on the rubble.

'Costello!' Gladwin screamed as she threw her torch to him.

Joe caught it just as the creature's head and torso hovered over him. Globules of black saliva dripped on Joe, eating through his clothes and into the skin underneath.

'I'm going to devour you whole, Costello!' the entity growled, its breath smelling like stale cigarette smoke. It then opened its mouth, expanding its snake-like jaws wide enough to bite off its prey's head in one mouthful.

Joe grimaced and snarled, 'Devour *this!*' He rammed the torch down the creature's gullet until his whole arm was deep inside the belly of the beast, and then he pressed the on button.

The creature screamed and Joe yanked his arm back; gaping black wounds, exposing the bone, ran the length of his forearm and the back of his hand.

The abomination reared up, writhing back and forth, thrashing against the walls. The blackness of its body began to lighten and turn grey; the tar-like texture began to set then became brittle, with fragments of it crumbling to the floor. It stood frozen like an ancient statue, but then Joe lifted his leg and kicked it dead centre in the chest. It exploded, blanketing Joe and Gladwin in dust and ash.

The torch fell to the floor with a clunk and, as the dust settled, the light flickered out, leaving the glow of the bulb's element to fade and die.

29

In the medical room, Linda bandaged Joe's arm then treated the wound across his stomach as best as she could. He winced when the duct tape pulled at the staples as his fiancée tore it away. The staples still held in place, but Joe would need a tetanus shot as soon as possible. Linda then placed a fresh bandage around his waist and held it in place with a safety pin.

Curtis lay on the bed nearby. Gladwin had given her a shot of morphine and tied a tourniquet around her thigh, just above the knee. It slowed the bleeding from her lower leg, but the muscle in her calf was completely destroyed. It was clear from the wounds she'd never be able to walk on it again. Gladwin didn't want to say anything just yet but she thought there was a strong possibility the leg would even need to be amputated.

For several minutes no one spoke. Joe held Linda in his arms, their eyes tightly shut as they enjoyed the comfort of the embrace. Gladwin stroked Curtis' head as she slept. Then Joe opened his eyes and lifted his head; as he did he noticed that the medicine bottles on the shelf opposite him were beginning to vibrate. The vibration became stronger, causing the bottles to move across the shelf and fall onto the floor, smashing into hundreds of pieces. The sound of the glass shattering caused Gladwin to look up.

The whole room now shook, so much so that it was difficult for them to stay on their feet. More bottles flew off the shelves, followed by books and other medical apparatus. Cracks began to appear in the wall and plaster fell from the ceiling.

'What the hell?' cried Gladwin, clutching a cabinet for support.

Joe looked at her, his eyes wide; a feeling in his gut gave him a suspicion as to what was happening. 'Barons!' he hissed.

From the commotion of the battle with the abomination, Gladwin had forgotten Barons was on the roof performing whatever ritual was required to get rid of the evil that threatened them. However, she also now had a feeling in the pit of her stomach that something wasn't right. She cursed herself for trusting Barons and leaving Officer Campbell alone with him.

She made her way across the room as best as she could, heading for the door, swaying left and right from the tremors. She didn't need to explain her actions; Joe knew exactly where she was going. 'I'm coming with you,' he said.

'Me too,' said Linda.

'No!' snapped Joe. He shook his head apologetically. 'I'm sorry, I didn't mean to... You would be much safer here.'

'And what about *you?*' Linda's bottom lip began to wobble. 'Who is going to keep you safe?'

'I really don't think this Barons is going to be too much trouble, even with that knife of his.'

'It's not the knife or him I'm worried about. It's those Shadowmen — the ones still out there.'

Joe stroked her cheek with the back of his hand and smiled, not noticing that the quake had now stopped. 'I'll be fine. Besides —' he nodded towards Curtis '— someone needs to keep an eye on her.'

Linda stood on her tiptoes and kissed Joe passionately. She licked her lips as she pulled away and then said, 'Go now, before I change my mind.'

Joe turned and left the room with Gladwin. Linda stood alone amongst the debris and began to sob.

30

The rain now eased off and the storm clouds dispersed. Once on the roof, the first thing they saw was Campbell lying face down. Barons was nowhere to be seen. Joe and Gladwin ran over to the fallen officer, but as they approached it was clear his throat had been slashed; the life had bled from him.

'I'm going to kill that son of a bitch for this!' Gladwin screamed. 'Where are you, Barons?!'

Joe held up his hand to silence her then pointed to the floor where Campbell lay. A humming sang from the circle that had been carved into the shingles. Each of the symbols within began to emit an orange glow and then cracks began to appear in the tiles within the circle. 'This can't be good,' he said, pulling Gladwin back.

Barons now appeared from behind the air vent where he had been hiding. 'You're just in time to witness my greatest achievement,' he said, and laughed, throwing his head back.

Then there was a huge explosion that sent shrapnel into the air. A piece of rubble caught Gladwin on the forehead, and the force knocked her and Joe several yards across the rooftop. Joe got to his feet and helped Gladwin up. Within the perimeter of the circle the roof had been blown wide open, but instead of seeing the rooms of the police station below there was nothing but a black void. Campbell's body slowly slipped over the edge and dropped into the abyss.

'You see, I needed blood to open the door,' shouted Barons as a cylinder of magenta light now shone out of the hole and into the night sky. Within the cylinder rings of white light began to pulsate upwards.

A north wind now began to blow, Joe and Gladwin shivered as the wind blew through their hair.

Black smoke began to bellow from the hole and spiral upwards like a tornado. Joe looked in horror as the truth of the situation fell upon him. 'Oh, fuck...' he whispered. These were the only words he could muster, for hundreds — no, *thousands* — of Shadowmen now swarmed into the night sky, eclipsing the moon.

* * *

Curtis began to stir. 'What happened?' she asked Linda, her throat dry and hoarse.

'Shh, just relax. You're going to be okay.'

Curtis looked around and then at her leg. 'That thing...'

'Dead. Or at least I hope so.'

Curtis lay her head back on the pillow and looked up at Linda. 'Where is everyone?'

'The roof. I think something important is happening up there.'

'Is Joe up there?'

Linda nodded.

'Then go!'

'But what about you?'

Curtis took hold of Linda's hand and squeezed it gently. 'I'll be fine. Go. He needs you.'

* * *

'You're free! My brothers and sisters, you are finally free!' shouted Barons, looking up at the swarm of Shadowmen that now occupied the sky above Raven's Peak.

Joe and Gladwin had taken cover behind one of the air vents as swarm after swarm spread across the night sky and some swooped down towards the streets of Raven's Peak.

'Now what?' Gladwin shouted over the cry of the wind and the screams of the Shadowmen.

'No clue!' Joe replied, gritting his teeth. 'Barons is the only one with the answers, and I don't think he's on the same team!'

They peered over the edge of the vent to see what Barons was doing; he appeared to be stood looking up at the swarms, talking to himself.

'It is done, my lord... Yes, I understand... My reward? What? No — but, I thought —'

Barons' entire body burst into flames, which were quickly quelled by the blowing hurricane. The antique knife he had been holding dropped to the floor and landed in a pile of ash. In Barons' wake stood a Shadowman. It screamed and then flew from the rooftop to join the swarms.

Joe and Gladwin ducked back behind the air vent. 'Now what?' the detective whispered desperately.

Joe shook his head. 'I have no...' He stopped, only now noticing the wound on Gladwin's forehead. 'You're bleeding.'

The detective touched the wound and rubbed the blood between her fingertips. 'Oh, that? It's just a scratch. A bit of debris caught me when the roof blew open. It's nothing.'

'It's blood.' Joe licked his lips and looked over the tornado of Shadowmen. 'It was always about blood...' He became lost in thought and then muttered, 'Blood is life.'

He fled the cover of the air vent and zigzagged his way across the roof top to where Barons had stood.

'Costello!' Gladwin screamed after him.

A Shadowman broke away from the swarm and swooped towards him. He ducked but the momentum of his run caused him to trip. Reacting quickly, he reached his arms out and rolled forward, avoiding the attack while taking hold of the knife as his body rotated. The Shadowman swooped again, but came to a halt when it saw what Joe was holding. Suddenly, it screamed and regrouped with the rest of the swarm.

'Costello, what are you doing?' Gladwin cried, her head peeping out from behind the air vent.

'Blood!' Joe called back as he sliced the palm of his hand with the blade. 'Barons said blood opened the door — maybe blood will close it!'

Blood flowed from the wound which he smeared over the length of the blade on both sides. His heart racing and lungs bursting, Joe slung the bloody blade into the void.

Nothing happened.

'Costello!' Gladwin shouted. He did not respond. 'Costello!' she called again.

Joe looked up, defeat showing clearly in his

eyes. Gladwin looked at him, equally disappointed.

'Joe,' she said, for the first time calling him by his preferred name, 'I think it's going to take something more than a few drops of blood to stop this.' She looked out across to the horizon, but the lights from the buildings and streets below could no longer be seen. As far as the eye could see there was nothing but Shadowmen.

Forlorn, Joe looked down at his feet, the wind blowing his hair and nipping at his ears and nose. Then he saw splatters of blood on the outside of the circle. It wasn't his; it was too old and dry. Joe guessed it belonged to Officer Campbell. Joe remembered how when they had first arrived on the rooftop they had found Campbell's dead body lying in the circle; it was only a few moments later that the roof exploded and all hell broke loose. Then Joe knew what needed to be done.

Joe turned his back to the tornado of Shadowmen and glanced at Gladwin. The look in her eyes told him she understood what he needed to do, but she still shook her head, unable to find any words. Joe shuffled back, his heels over the edge of the precipice. Then he stepped forward, trembling. He was scared and angry that this was his only option. He stamped his feet and pounded his fists against his head. Grinding his teeth together in frustration, he yelled, 'Damn you all!'

He took a deep breath to steady himself but he could not control his trembling limbs. His stomach knotted. He wanted to throw up. The lump in his throat felt like he had swallowed a golf ball as he tried to hold back his tears. Then he remembered his first encounter with the abomination and what it had told him. Joe acknowledged its words were true. He had been afraid, afraid of becoming his father. The sudden realisation of this fear was like a weight being lifted. He felt free. Feeling calmer now, he shuffled back towards the edge.

At that moment Linda burst through the access door and saw her fiancé standing on the edge of the abyss, his arms outstretched. She screamed his name and sped towards him. Gladwin tried to grab hold of her, but Linda slipped through her grasp. Joe saw his fiancée running towards him and a tear now rolled down his cheek. 'I'm sorry,' he whispered. He closed his eyes, leaned backwards and vanished into the blackness of the tornado.

Linda screamed and sobbed as Gladwin took hold of her suddenly limp body and pulled her back behind the air vent. There was a surge of blue lightning within the swarm and then the tornado stopped spiralling clockwise and began to swirl in the opposite direction. The wind also changed direction, and instead of blowing in their faces it began to blow from behind. The growing tornado began to pull the swarms back in towards it. Once caught in the eye of the storm the legions of Shadowmen swirled down the funnel, being forced back into the hole like water running down the drain. The waves of light that had pulsated upward now began to flow down, sucking the remainder of the Shadowmen back into the void. With the last of the Shadowmen gone, the magenta light ceased. There was a sudden blinding flash, causing Linda and Gladwin to cover their eyes. The wind dropped and then there was silence.

Gladwin opened her eyes and looked around the rooftop. The hole had been filled. All that remained as evidence of the horrible events were the markings that Barons had scratched into the shingles.

'Linda,' she whispered, 'it's over.'

Linda opened her eyes and looked around. 'Joseph!' She jumped up and ran to the circle. Gladwin chased after her. Sparks of electricity flowed around the edge of the circle and died as Linda approached. There was no sign of Joe.

She dropped to her knee and began to pull up the shingles, breaking her nails and slicing the tips of her fingers as she did so. Her efforts were in vain, as there was nothing beneath but floorboards. Hysterical, she began to pound at the floor, screaming and kicking. Her chest constricted and her heart felt as though it had exploded into a million fragments.

Gladwin knelt down next to her and cradled her head against her chest as Linda wept.

31

The sun began to rise the following morning and rays of light flooded the foyer, causing it to warm up like a greenhouse. Soon the engineering team arrived and were able to force the automatic doors open, which were the only entrance and exit to the Raven's Peak police station. The team was shortly followed by the superintendent and several officers. The super had a multitude of questions for the most senior officer on site. By default, it fell to Detective Inspector Sarah Gladwin to answer.

Gladwin was suspended from active duty while an investigation into the incident took place. The three-month investigation was eventually brought to a close due to the number of complaints from the families of the deceased (although many victims were officially classed as missing, presumed dead) who wanted to try to move on with their lives.

Once she returned to duty, Gladwin was transferred to Bradford South and even received a promotion to the serious crimes unit.

As Gladwin had predicted, Officer Stacey Curtis lost her left leg. She received a generous sum of compensation from the police, who also paid for private medical care and rehabilitation. This was, however, under the proviso that she did not speak of the matter to any third parties.

A joint funeral service was held for Officer

James Campbell, Officer Jake Carpenter, Officer Benjamin Raimi, Officer Nathan Craven, Officer Richard Englund and Sergeant David Crompton. However, out of these only remains of Carpenter were recovered.

Detective Chief Inspector Francis Wilson's funeral service was held privately at the request of his mother. A joint service was held for him and his younger brother Michael Wilson. But, as was the case with many of the Shadowmen's victims, his body was not found. His empty coffin was buried alongside his brother's.

No next of kin could be traced for Adam Barons, and if his name hadn't been logged on the station's register no one would have really known he was missing. As a formality a small service was held with only a few officials in attendance.

Charles MacDonald and the others who had gone missing within Druid Wood received private services with only family members in attendance.

As with the Wilson brothers, a joint service was held for the Costellos, but, again, there were no bodies to bury. Linda read a eulogy for both Joe and Tony, as their mother was too distraught to do so.

For the first three months following the funeral Linda would visit Joe's grave every day. As time moved on this became a few times a week then once a week, usually on a Saturday. After April of the following year visits at the most were monthly.

It was now early November and Linda stood at Joe and Tony's graves. She had cleared the wilted flowers left by the last visitor, most likely their mother, and left fresh ones. She left a white lily on Tony's grave, but would always place a red carnation on Joe's. It was the first and only flower he had ever bought her.

She said a small prayer and turned to leave. Suddenly, she spotted the silhouette of someone sulking amongst the trees at the opposite end of the cemetery. The shape and the way in which it moved reminded Linda of someone she had once known. Her lip wobbled and a tear welled up in her eye. 'Joseph?' she whispered in disbelief, squinting and raising a hand to block the sun from her eyes. She was sure it was him. 'Joseph?!'

She ran over to the trees. The figure was startled but, as she approached, it reluctantly stepped out of the shadows.

It wasn't Joe.

The man looked very much like Joe but must have been some twenty years older. His hair had once been the same jet black colour but was now grey and thinning. The man, while holding a similar build to Joe, was not in shape. His size came from years of drink rather than exercise. 'Sorry, I didn't mean to frighten you, Miss Williams,' he said with a slight Italian accent.

'How did you know…?'

'Sorry, miss. Let me introduce myself. I'm Giuseppe Costello, but everyone calls me Gus.' He held out a hand.

Linda looked at it for a moment then reluctantly shook it.

'My boys are buried over there, aren't they?'

Linda nodded and they walked over to the gravestones.

Gus knelt down and touched each of the stones in turn, starting with Joe's. His eyes closed tightly. 'They were good boys, you know.'

Linda smiled. 'The best.'

Gus Costello stood up and wiped a small tear from his eye. 'I read in the paper they didn't find their bodies. Is that right? Did you see my boys die?'

She bit her lips as a pang of grief stung her. 'I don't really know what happened to Tony.' She shook her head and took a deep breath in an attempt to control her emotions. 'To be honest, I don't really know what happened to Joseph. I didn't see him die, as such. He was there and then... Oh God, I don't know!'

Gus held up a hand and hushed her. 'You and Joe were to be married, yes?'

Linda nodded. 'Today would have been our first wedding anniversary.'

Gus smiled and Linda's heart drummed. He had the same smile as Joe. 'I wasn't there for my boys when I should have been, and now it's too late. But let me try and make it up in some way. I think maybe I could be your friend — that might be a good start.'

She gave another nod. 'Okay, I'd like that.'

'Let me start by buying my daughter-in-law a coffee.'

They linked arms and headed towards the cemetery gates. As they left, Gus said, 'I don't want to give you false hope, but you know... no bodies. The way I see it, unless there is an actual body, how does anyone really know a person is dead? You never know, eh?'

Linda didn't answer, but a weak smile graced her lips.

EPILOGUE

All around was blackness as he fell. There was not a single ray of sunshine or the glow of streetlamp or silver of moonlight. His gut told him he wasn't blind. Here, in this place, light simply did not exist.

He couldn't tell how long he had been falling; like the light, time did not exist. It felt he had been falling for an eternity, yet in the blink of an eye he now hit the ground.

Joe dug his fingers into what felt like ice-cold dirt as he coughed and spluttered from trying to catch the air that had been knocked out of him. He coughed again as he breathed in the sulphurous, noxious air. A bitter wind blew around him; every hair stood on end as his skin broke out in goosebumps.

In the distance Joe could hear the tortured cries of men, women and children creating a chorus of thousands of woeful souls.

Joe opened his eyes and found he could now see clearly, but he was unsure what was illuminating his surroundings as the sky above him was black and starless. The ground on which he stood was made of cold red sand, and behind him stretched a canyon of the same colour. A few feet ahead, a river flowed. It was also red, but a deeper, browner shade. Joe neared it and there was a metallic taste in the air.

His eyes followed the direction in which the

river flowed. In the distance there appeared to be some kind of settlement or fort — the gates to a city, perhaps? This was also the home of the screams.

Taking all this in, Joe was left confused and afraid. 'What the hell?'

Perhaps a more apt question would have been, 'Where in Hell?'

AUTHOR PROFILE

Duncan Thompson has spent most of his life in a small market town in West Yorkshire — the same town in which most of his stories are set under the guise of Raven's Peak. Duncan has been writing works of fiction since the age of seven. In those early days, his stories often involved himself and his friends being transported to fantasy worlds. However, as a teenager, Duncan fell in love with horror movies and his writing took a whole new direction.

His debut book, *Within the Dark Places*, was intended to be a standalone novel. However, while halfway through the various drafts, Duncan had a dream involving the hero he had created and felt the urge to write about it. Consequently, *Where the Darkness Hides* was born.

Duncan works in financial services and lives with his partner and their two young children. He is currently working on a new project exploring the lives of the various residents of Raven's Peak and the paranormal incidents that take place there, and he says this isn't the last we have seen of the Shadowmen.

Publisher Information

Rowanvale Books provides publishing services to independent authors, writers and poets all over the globe. We deliver a personal, honest and efficient service that allows authors to see their work published, while remaining in control of the process and retaining their creativity. By making publishing services available to authors in a cost-effective and ethical way, we at Rowanvale Books hope to ensure that the local, national and international community benefits from a steady stream of good quality literature.

For more information about us, our authors or our publications, please get in touch.

www.rowanvalebooks.com
info@rowanvalebooks.com

Lightning Source UK Ltd.
Milton Keynes UK
UKOW02f0214170317
296834UK00001B/5/P